UP A TREE

"Joey, how come you're in the tree?" I bellowed.

I heard silence except for the sound of birds shifting on the branches and a little breeze that tickled the spring leaves. I begged, "Joey, come on down." The breeze whipped into a strong wind.

"I'm going to live up here forever," he retorted adamantly.

"How are you going to eat? Sleep?" I hated to miss a meal and sleep was heaven! And even if I brought him grub every day, Joey risked falling off the platform. We had built it so long ago maybe the nails had begun to loosen.

Joey maintained that he wasn't hungry and would never be hungry again. He had been humiliated in front of a special girl. According to him, she was probably snickering behind her dainty little hands at that very moment.

As Joey got sadder, I stoked the fires of anger. That fatso coach had slandered my best friend. It hurt not only him, but me, too, because weren't we almost the same? After all, weren't we separated by only a couple of streets? Wasn't his birthday in April, just like mine, and didn't we both like the gymnast girl?

"Don't worry," I told Joey.

gary soto

Mercy on These Teenage Chimps

Harcourt, Inc.

Orlando   Austin   New York   San Diego   London

www.HarcourtBooks.com

First Harcourt paperback edition 2008

The Library of Congress has cataloged the hardcover edition as follows:
Soto, Gary.
Mercy on these teenage chimps/Gary Soto.
p.   cm.
Summary: At thirteen years old, best friends Ronnie and Joey suddenly
feel like chimps—long armed, big eared, and gangly—and when the
coach humiliates Joey in front of a girl, he climbs up a tree and refuses
to come down.
[1. Best friends—Fiction. 2. Friendship—Fiction. 3. Coming of age—
Fiction. 4. Puberty—Fiction.] I. Title.
PZ7.S7242Me   2007
[Fic]—dc22   2006002599
ISBN 978-0-15-206022-0
ISBN 978-0-15-206215-6 pb

Text set in Minister Light
Designed by April Ward

DOM 10 9 8 7 6 5 4 3
4500242839
Printed in the United States of America

To **Linda Jabara**
and **Dora Maher,**
librarians and friends
in the good cause

Mercy
on These
Teenage
Chimps

Chapter 1

I, Ronaldo Gonzalez, better known as Ronnie, was like any other boy until I turned thirteen and woke up as a chimpanzee. I examined my reflection in the bathroom mirror. What was this? The peachy fuzz on my chin? The splayed ears? The wide grin that revealed huge teeth? I played with my mouth, squeezing it as I had seen the chimpanzees do on *Animal Planet*, my favorite TV channel. I wiggled my ears. My nose appeared flatter than ever.

Mom noticed the change right away. Instead of eggs, bacon, and buttered toast, my usual morning pick-me-up, I had a bowl of Froot Loops and a banana, but not before I juggled three apples and a single orange. I seemed to have been charged with an uncanny ability to keep things in the air.

"What's gotten into you?" She laughed. "You should be in the circus!"

"It's my birthday," I answered. I was glad that I had been born in spring. Spring was when the mountains appeared majestically in the distance and retirees got out their mowers to clobber the first dandelions sprouting on their lawns. Spring was when birds and flowers did their magic of lifting the souls of regular people.

I could see Mom registering in her mind that I was no longer a kid. She pulled at my cheek tenderly and told me that I was a young man and that soon she would lose me to some trashy girl. Of course, I promised never to move away and that the trashy girl could come live with us.

Mom playfully spanked my bottom thirteen times, my new age, and then asked me if I had hurt my leg. She had noticed that my gait seemed wider and was sort of rolling. She also inquired about my arms. They were hanging so low at my side that I could tie my shoes without bending over.

"Nah, Mom," I answered. "I'm okay."

That morning I felt curiously different, and even older when Mom let me sit at the head of the kitchen table—ever since Dad had taken off, his place usually held piles of clean laundry. And that's what I did that morning. I accepted my position as head of the table, whipping out the newspaper and muttering to myself that the San Francisco Giants were already four behind the Los Angeles Dodgers.

I was suddenly a teenage chimp. My best friend, Joey Rios, a few days older than me, had also turned into a chimp. For years we had been just like other boys—muddy, with scabs on our knees and elbows—until we both had growth spurts. Our arms, it seemed, hung a few inches longer and our ears sprung out from the sides of our heads. We caught ourselves beating our chests and jumping, especially Joey, who was a wrestler. Each time he pinned an opponent he'd jump up and down and circle the mat, pacing off his territory. He just couldn't help himself.

And how we could climb! Joey and I often scaled the tall tree in front of his house, where we sat for hours. Most of our talk involved girls and food. We avoided talking about our looks, as we were doubtful that we were handsome. Indeed, I sometimes played a refrain in my mind: *We ugly, we real ugly.*

"Do you know the meaning of life?" On my birthday I'd asked Joey this question thirty feet up, with a chimp's view of our small-town neighborhood.

"Not a bit," Joey answered. He pursed his lips,

spat at the ground, and wiped his mouth with the back of his hand. "Except I know spit takes three seconds to hit my cat."

His cat looked around, mystified by the sudden presence of rain.

"Do you think any girls will like us?"

Joey didn't answer. He just spat again, and again his cat, none too smart, looked around until a sparrow caught his attention. He pranced after the sparrow, who, blessed with keen sight and swift wings, lifted up and away.

A week later we were policing our school for the usual litter of potato chip bags, candy wrappers, and soda cups. We had detention for being tardy— on the way to school, we had stopped to swing on the monkey bars at the public playground.

"This is way nasty," I groaned, wincing at the sight of a swollen hot dog. I poked it with a stick and deposited it in a plastic trash bag. It was a sickening sight. We were non-meat eaters, devoted vegetarians who loved fruits and veggies, plus what my mom called "monkey juice," the fruity smoothies I concocted in the blender.

"Who's this?" Joey held up a photo he had found on the ground.

We studied the photo, our heads nearly touching. "She's pretty," I said longingly. Then, *We ugly, we real ugly,* repeated in my mind. The pang was like a fishhook in my heart.

Joey dropped the photo into his trash bag, and we continued with our task until we saw, in the distance, Coach Puddlefield approaching. Every dozen or so steps he slowed to hike up his pants—he was a big man whose stomach cast a shadow in front of him. Behind his back, we students called him Coach Bear. He was way hairy and growled a lot.

Coach Bear chugged across the lawn. "You two monkeys," he bellowed. "I got a job for you."

The last time Coach Bear had required our service was to put all the balls away in the gymnasium. Joey, an occasional show-off, had spotted a volleyball in the rafters. He spat into his hands and climbed the bleachers, pushed himself up on the window ledge, grabbed and swung from the exercise rope, shimmied up the rope, and boosted himself up onto an iron girder. Then his fingers tickled the ball from where it was caught behind the rafter. Coach had yelled at him for risking his neck, but Joey was just doing what any chimp would have done.

Now it seemed that Coach Bear required our

services again. He halted in front of us, giving his pants one final tug. He wiped his brow with a thick finger.

"We're already doing something, Coach," Joey explained.

"And what is that, exactly?"

"Picking up litter," I said, jiggling the contents of the plastic trash bag. "We have detention."

Coach Bear sniffed. "You guys been eating hot dogs?"

"No, sir," Joey answered.

"We're vegetarians," I divulged. I had studied the diets and life spans of carnivores and noncarnivores, and was prepared to offer a litany of reasons why a person, young or old, skinny or fat, boy or girl, should avoid meat like the plague.

"Vegetarians! No wonder you boys are so skinny. Not you, Rios." Coach Bear corrected himself, as he was proud of Joey, the wrestler. Joey was anything but a weakling. The previous year he had captured the regional championship, and Coach had a soft spot for champions. Then his eyes slid over to me, and he held his tongue, which was muscled from yelling at kids for a dozen or so years. "Anyhow, I'm here to ask if you guys could help out with a banquet tonight. I need two more kids, and if you do it you can quit the trash pickup." He told us that the regional sports awards banquet would be held at the high school down the street.

Joey turned to me. I wiggled my ears as an affirmative yes.

"What are we supposed to wear?" Joey asked.

Coach Bear scratched his forehead thoughtfully. "A clean white shirt."

Joey, biting his lower lip, hesitated and asked, "Do we wear pants?"

Coach Bear beaded his eyes at Joey, who released a smile. "Just kidding, Coach."

Coach Bear instructed us to get there by five thirty, hiked up his pants as he turned, and sized up trouble on another part of the school grounds. He waved a paw at two kids trying to shimmy up a drainpipe.

"You knuckleheads," he roared. "Get off of there!"

I knew the culprits. I poked at a candy wrapper and mused how in a year, two years at most, those boys would wake up as chimpanzees.

It was just a matter of time.

Chapter 2

Later, dressed in white shirts and black pants, Joey and I biked over to Lincoln High School. Actually, Joey pedaled and I rode the handlebars, the prow of the bicycle. From that princely height, I felt exhilarated as the wind blew through my hair, narrowed my eyes, pinned back my ears, and rushed down my throat until I could hardly breathe.

"Hold on," Joey warned.

We were full of springtime joy. More than once I grinned at a neighbor seated on a porch taking in the last rays of the day. I smiled at the tidy gardens and the birds yanking up worms from lawns spongy from last week's rain. Life seemed immeasurably good. Not a single pooch ran after us, snapping its frothy teeth at our ankles.

At Lincoln we locked the bike in a bike stall,

pushed our shirttails back into our pants, and entered the gymnasium.

"Over here!" Coach Bear called. His neck was choked by a reddish tie that lay on his large belly like a length of spaghetti.

We hurried over.

"Did you wash your hands?" Coach Bear asked as he smoothed a tablecloth.

"Yes, sir," I answered.

Coach Bear narrowed his eyes at me. "When?"

"Today," I answered.

"Get your paws washed in the faculty bathroom." The faculty john was off-limits to students, except when time was precious, it seemed. "And hurry up!"

We disappeared down the hall to the faculty bathroom. Joey and I washed our hands and then sprayed our necks with orange-scented air freshener.

"How do we smell?" I asked.

Joey's nostrils worked the air. "Fruity," he assessed. He surveyed the faculty bathroom and concluded that it was nice. He pointed out a deodorant gizmo wired to the toilet bowl. He flushed the toilet and remarked, "It smells good. Way better than the boys' room."

We returned to the gymnasium.

"What do we do, Coach?" Joey asked.

Coach Bear told us to unfold the folding chairs and place six at each table. We soon completed that task. He next told us to blow up balloons, attach a string to the navel of each, and tape a balloon to the center of each tablecloth. It would add a festive mood, especially with the splash of glitter that Coach Bear had already sprinkled on the tables.

"You can do this, can't you?" Coach Bear asked as we sauntered over to a small cylinder filled with helium. "You think you can fill 'em up without busting 'em?"

"Yeah," we both sang gleefully.

"Show me."

I took a balloon, stretched it like taffy, and hooked it on the hose that snaked from the cylinder. I turned the valve and the balloon quickly filled up like the fat cheeks of a huge man.

"Don't make them so big!" Coach Bear growled.

"We won't," I replied. "That was just the practice one." I began to preach that practice makes perfect, certain that on the field Coach spouted such wisdom. But he told me to shut my trap and threatened to send us higher than a balloon if we dared to inhale any of the helium. He warned us that he would check on us every few minutes to see if our voices sounded weirdly high.

After Coach Bear left, Joey and I began filling balloons. Joey enjoyed a better touch working the valve, but I was a pro at lassoing the string to the balloon—we were a good team. Soon we had twenty balloons clutched in our hands like flowers. Next, we taped the balloons to the tablecloths. We stepped back and appraised our work.

"It looks really cool, huh?" Joey remarked.

"Right on!" But I observed that the balloon on table fourteen—each table held a stick with a number—was misbehaving. It had already begun to droop.

I replaced that balloon with a new one and beamed with pride at our handiwork.

"You know what kind of grub they're serving?" Joey wondered aloud. He placed a hand on his stomach to tame its growling. The food had been on my mind, too. I sniffed the air and didn't smell anything but orange-scented air freshener.

But we didn't dwell long on the food because Coach Bear approached us and gruffly asked if we had been inhaling the helium. We shook our heads.

"Say something," he said. He was suspicious.

"Like what?" I asked.

"Like what grade you're in!"

"We're in seventh grade," I answered.

"Next year we'll be in eighth grade," Joey added with a goofy smile.

Coach Bear was satisfied that we hadn't been mischievously sucking on the helium hose, but still he claimed that we had girl voices. He predicted that by next year our voices would break and we would sound the way boys are supposed to sound. Then he told us to staple the evening's program.

We accepted our new job and began to fold the photocopied programs and shoot their spines with staples.

"Look!" Joey cried.

I looked around.

"No, here!" Joey pointed out two wrestlers in the program. "I wrestled this one," he said. "I pinned him in nineteen seconds."

"What took you so long?" I joked. But I quit joking when I measured Joey's sadness. Joey, last year a champion wrestler, had been banned from the team because of his antics after each victory. He had already been acting chimplike—beating his chest, jumping up and down, and letting out his primordial chimp scream. The other schools wouldn't have it.

"I could have been honored tonight," Joey said wistfully.

"Ah, Joey, it's no big deal." I offered to be his practice dummy if he wanted to keep up wrestling on his own. I promised to go down in less than nineteen seconds. He could even jump on my chest if he felt so inclined.

"You're the best friend ever," Joey claimed. He poked a finger around his eye and felt for a tear. He found only sleep and a dab of moisture. Still, he meant it. Ronnie was the best friend ever.

Eventually the first honorees and their guests— mainly parents with circles under their eyes from working long hours—began to arrive. Soon we discovered that only cookies and punch were being served. Joey and I were presented with white gloves to wear while we passed the trays of refreshments.

"But we washed our hands already," I argued.

Coach Bear glowered at me. He told me that I had been touching stuff and that maybe some germs were on the tips of my fingers. He asked how I would like it if some monkey kids like us were serving food when just a few minutes ago they'd been scratching an armpit or maybe using a fingernail to poke at foodstuff on a dirty tooth.

"We wouldn't like it at all," Joey volunteered.

I agreed with Joey. Why debate the matter? Coach Bear's fur would bristle and his hollering would fill the cavities of our ears if we didn't heed his suggestion. He was under pressure to make the awards banquet a success. I slipped on the white gloves, hiked up my pants, and maneuvered through the thickening crowd with a tray of cookies. Joey, the one of us with better balance, had hoisted a large platter onto his shoulder. He shadowed my steps, calling out, "Punch, anybody. Tasty punch."

We circulated with our sugary provisions and soon returned to our workstation to replenish our supplies. It was then that Joey punched me in the arm, beckoning for my full attention, or as much as I could give with my mouth stuffed with cookies.

"Did you see her?" Joey whispered.

I looked about, confused. I mumbled, "See who?" I swallowed my cookie, cleared my throat, and asked again, "See who?"

"*Her!*" He pointed to a pretty girl whose face was as sweetly pink as our punch. She was dressed in a pink dress and her knees were pink, too.

"Adorable," I agreed. Truthfully, my tongue was too busy working a cookie into a delicious paste to be impressed. But Joey, I could see, was smitten big time.

"I wonder who she is," Joey said dreamily. "I've never seen her at our school."

"Let's go find out," I said.

I scooped cookies onto my platter, and Joey splashed a new round of drinks into clear cups. We hurried over, glad that we had not only washed our hands but also misted ourselves with air freshener. We needed all the help we could get.

"Punch!" Joey crowed brightly.

The girl, alone at the moment, whirled around.

"No, thank you," she said with a beauty queen's wave of the hand. But she offered us a smile and looped her hair behind her ears.

"I'm Joey Rios," Joey said. "And this is my best friend, Ronnie Gonzalez. We go to Washington Middle School."

The girl blinked at us.

I could see that Joey, the less experienced of the two of us when it came to girls, was faltering badly. She was cute, this much I admit, and I scolded myself for giving so much attention to the cookie I had been pulverizing a few minutes earlier. What was wrong with me?

Because my best friend had been kicked off the wrestling squad and wasn't being honored that evening—the unfairness!—I was committed to helping him succeed. I picked up for him and added, "We had detention today, but Coach is letting us work off our time by helping tonight."

I recounted the history of our tardiness and the

bike ride over to Lincoln. I forged ahead with a lot of sentences, mentioning Joey, my happy-go-lucky chimp friend, as much as I could. I tried to exude nice vibes, and Joey then jumped in and informed this girl that we were wrist deep in white gloves because no one could tell where germs lurked. Germs didn't have faces, he added philosophically, but if they did they would be really ugly faces. *Joey*, I thought, *don't demonstrate*.

"Like this," Joey said. He scrunched up his face into a version of ugliness, arguing that that was what a germ might look like under a microscope. He then advanced his theory about germs. Although no scientist, he believed that they could get hold of you, bend you this way and that way, and lay you low for weeks.

"Enough, Joey," I butted in. I shifted the conversation to the adorable girl. "How come you're here?"

"I'm being honored," she replied. "For gymnastics. I took third in the state championships. I've been practicing since I was six. I'm on the team at Adams Middle School."

"Like, wow," Joey crowed.

"Like ditto wow," I responded gleefully. Not only was she pretty, but she could tumble, do splits, and vault onto the beam without banging her head. I was impressed.

"Joey used to wrestle," I said, patting my friend's rock-hard shoulders.

Joey grinned.

"He used to be really, really good."

Joey's smile lost its luster, though, when she asked, "You aren't wrestling anymore?"

"He hurt his back," I answered anxiously. I was filled with more hot air than the balloons hovering over the tables. I concocted a story about how Joey had lost a bunch of weight and then had to put that weight back on. His vegetarianism had affected his equilibrium. His opponent was none other than a state wrestling champ called Igor, who a few months before had become addicted to white powdered doughnuts. Joey had pinned this flabby state wrestler just seconds after the bell gonged.

The girl's hands came together and applauded.

"Ronnie is exaggerating," Joey said. He was touched by my fabrication.

I didn't have time to build on this story because across the gymnasium Coach Bear was weaving between the guests like a football player through defenders. He was headed toward us.

"Congratulations," I stuttered to the girl, and

pulled on Joey's arm. We had to get back to plying the guests with sweets. "What's your name?"

"Jessica." She covered her mouth as she laughed. Why she was laughing was a mystery. Maybe she was just happy.

Joey and I made our exit. But Coach Bear tracked us down and warned us not to mingle with the guests. We were the refreshment crew, as well as the two knuckleheads who would sweep up afterward.

"Right," Joey said, bowing slightly.

But just as we started to again spread the gospel of cookies and punch, the master of ceremonies tapped the microphone with a finger. Lights dimmed. Latecomers hurried to their seats. The awards ceremony began with the Pledge of Allegiance. Then the crowd was dazzled by a six-year-old baton twirler, and next was moved by the testimony of a college basketball player whose life had turned around when he discovered that he wasn't starter material after all. He had learned that it was okay to sit on the bench. What mattered was that he had made the team and got to know some interesting people.

The individual awards began. The audience applauded for a long-distance runner, two swimmers, a tackle, a quarterback whose neck was propped up by a brace, a skateboarder with punched-out knees, and a forward on the regional soccer championship team. When Jessica's name was announced, Joey and I leaped to our feet, applauding wildly.

As she rose and acknowledged the applause with a big smile, the balloon at her table wiggled free from its tape and started a slow climb toward the ceiling. I followed its flight and was thinking, *Oh, well, that one's lost.* But was I wrong. Joey stripped his gloves from his hands and leaped up on the bleachers. Before anyone could tell what was happening, he was up on the ledge of a tall bank of windows.

"Careful, Joey," I muttered. I was touched by his chivalry, and then mad for not thinking of it first— shoot, I could have been the hero. I envisioned Joey capturing the balloon from the rafters; scaling down the side of the wall (notched with bolts for an easy descent); and on one knee, returning the prize to Jessica. But this image popped like a balloon when I heard Coach Bear's blaring voice.

"Mr. Rios!"

Coach Bear had taken over at the podium. His eyes flashed as he gripped the microphone and ordered, "Get down from there!"

Joey scurried across the rafters toward the balloon, which had nested in a joint. He snatched the string and straddled a girder. The audience gasped.

"In a minute," Joey bellowed from a tremendous height.

"Get down! You're gonna give me a heart attack." Coach Bear's anger had undone the noose of his tie.

Joey fiddled with something and patted at the balloon, which began to descend. Anchoring it was a badminton shuttlecock, lost up there for years and smartly put to use as a weight.

Spritelike, Jessica danced toward the descending balloon and caught it in her palms like a bouquet. She smiled at Joey's valiant gesture.

I would have been jealous right on the spot— *God, Joey thinks of everything!*—except for what Coach Bear yelled next.

"Who do you think you are? A monkey?"

Chapter 3

Words do hurt. Joey climbed meekly from the rafters to face Coach Bear, who yelled at him in front of Jessica and a whole load of people, some of whom had returned to munching cookies and gulping punch. Joey's face drooped like an old heavy sunflower and his shoulders slumped. And was that a tear that splashed between his shoes?

"But Coach, that's unfair!" I stepped in to defend Joey's gallant actions. Couldn't Coach see why Joey had risked himself? I assumed that he was married and familiar with love—wasn't that a dull wedding band embedded on his furry finger? But Coach roasted my ears with hurtful words.

I could only take so much. I peeled off my gloves and tossed them over my shoulder. A girl caught them.

"We're gone! We're out of here!" I yelled back. I was upset, but I pledged to worry about the consequences only when we got back to school on Monday. The weekend was ahead of us.

"You're going to clean up first!"

"No, we're not!" I replied heatedly.

We departed in spite of Coach's threats that we would get lifetime detention and that he would make us run laps until we were skin and bones. We rode home in silence. I didn't bark out in pain when the bike dipped into potholes—the handlebars were a cruel ending to a cruel evening. The ride ended at my front lawn with Joey claiming that maybe he belonged in a tree.

"What are you talking about?" I asked.

"I'm just a monkey, like Coach said."

"No you're not. If you're anything, you're a chimp. Where's your dignity?"

Joey swiveled his bike around and propelled himself away.

Before I went inside—my mother was on the couch laughing at a comedy on television—I sadly dwelled on our lowly status as teenage chimps. I sat on the front step and meditated on the stars shifting ever so slightly in the wide night sky. The moon was creeping up. A neighbor's bathroom light went on and seconds later his toilet flushed. A cat prowled in the bushes that separated our yard from the neighbor's yard.

I was thirteen, a chimp by all appearances. What would the stars bring me? A good education? A day job? A chimp girl all my own? I lowered my head and tried to cry a few tears, but nothing would come out.

The next morning I called Joey. His mother informed me that Joey had climbed into the tree in front of their house, and it was fine by her. She wanted him out of the house so she could do some spring cleaning.

I jumped into my clothes, unzipped three bananas with a fingernail, devoured them while I made my bed, and rode my skateboard to Joey's house. Sure enough, Joey was nesting in the tree in front of his house, the same tree where we had built a little platform when we were eight. I shaded my eyes with my hand and circled the trunk. I could see his legs, but nothing else.

"Joey, how come you're in the tree?" I bellowed.

I heard silence except for the sound of birds shifting on the branches and a little breeze that tickled the spring leaves. I begged, "Joey, come on down." The breeze whipped into a strong wind for a brief second.

Joey's mother appeared on the porch. She wore a crown of pink curlers that matched her pink slippers.

"See," she yelled. "He likes it better up there!" She asked me what had happened that would make him skip breakfast and go up a tree.

I shrugged. I wasn't about to spill the beans about Joey falling in love or how he had risked his life to rescue a balloon from the rafters.

After Joey's mother returned inside, I shimmied up the tree. It wasn't much work because I was used to conquering heights. In fact, Joey and I had once scurried up the fifty-foot pine tree at the court-house park.

"Come on, Joey," I begged as I placed an arm on his shoulder.

He sniffed and wiped his nose. He grumbled that maybe stupid Coach Bear was right.

"Trees are for birds," I argued. I spied the wooden bones of a kite that probably belonged to Joey. "Plus kites."

"I'm going to live up here forever," he retorted adamantly.

"How are you going to eat? Sleep?" I hated to miss a meal and sleep was heaven! And even if I brought him grub every day, Joey risked falling off the platform. We had built it so long ago maybe the nails had begun to loosen.

Joey maintained that he wasn't hungry and would never be hungry again. He had been humiliated in front of a special girl. According to him, she was probably snickering behind her pretty little hands at that very moment.

"She would never do that!"

"How do you know?"

"I just do. She's too nice to laugh at someone's pain."

For a brief moment, my concern for my friend vanished when I noticed a line of ants on a far limb. What were they doing way up here? I had suposed that ants were trekkers of loose soil, flowers, and dropped soda bottles. What could they find useful in a tree where a sad boy was absently peeling bark?

"Coach was mean," Joey babbled. His eyes darkened with tears.

"He was, like, way mean!" I agreed and pounded my fist on my thigh. "I'm never going to inflate balloons for him again!"

As Joey got sadder, I stoked the fires of anger. That fatso coach had slandered my best friend. It hurt not only him, but me, too, because weren't we almost the same? After all, weren't we separated by only a couple of streets? Wasn't his birthday in April, just like mine, and didn't we both like this gymnast girl? Of course, I would dutifully step aside to let my pained friend pursue her.

"Don't worry," I told Joey.

"What do I have to worry about? My life is over." He tore a leaf from the tree and blew his nose into it. He let the leaf go, and it fell with the weight of tears and snot.

After I left my buddy, I resolved to play Cupid. I had to find Jessica, bathe her ears with sweet sounds, and at close range plug her with a couple of arrows. Injured by love—for I would really pull back far on the bow—she would hurry over and entice Joey from the tree with tender words. But where did she live? I had no map, no hints. She had to be somewhere in Pinkerton. I imagined her doing cartwheels on her front lawn, a locket around her neck bouncing like crazy. After all, the day was pretty nice. Folks were out enjoying the rays, doing home projects in garages, and crunching snails in flower beds.

Our area has one high school, two middle schools, and four elementary schools. We can ride our bikes to the town limits and view fields of grapes, cotton, and sugar beets. There we can pet the large heads of cows and offer straw to perpetually famished goats. On windy days, we can hear music coming from beyond the coastal range, but we never get to go there. Our small town has a water tower painted with PINKERTON and, occasionally, bad words scratched by sullen boys.

"I got to find her," I said aloud.

Adams Middle School was across town. I rode my skateboard in that direction, paying no attention when Cory, a gap-toothed boy who used to thrash me weekly until Joey came to my defense, saw me go by and called me monkey face. I had a bigger calling than to stop and debate his taunts.

I skidded to a halt in front of Adams. The school was just as sorry as ours. The grass was chewed up from students playing tackle football. A window was boarded up. The V on the vice principal's door was missing. Pushed by wind, litter crawled down the open hallway, where, in the eaves, wasps hummed and stitched frightful nests. I propelled my skateboard down the hall and stopped at the drinking fountain. As at our school, this one dribbled pitifully. I pursed my lips and did my best to quench my thirst.

I spotted three girls out near the baseball diamond. They had hula hoops spinning on their skinny hips. Their hoop earrings swung with each gyration.

"Hey," I called.

The hula hoops slowed until they dropped to the ground.

"You know this girl…," I started. I decided to throw a wide net out there.

The girls looked at one another and whispered.

"Does she have monkey ears like you do?" one asked.

I ignored her smirk. "This girl does gymnastics and she's really good. She goes to this school, I think."

"We're going to call the police if you don't leave us alone," the smirky girl warned.

"Do your arms always hang down like that?" the smallest of the three asked, meaning below my knees. She had brought the hula hoop back up around her waist and was churning away.

I propped my hands on my hips and muttered darkly, "They look cute, but they're way mean." I rolled away with my head high. As Cupid I had to be noble in trying to locate Jessica. What mattered was making my friend happy.

The school was pretty empty on a Saturday, so I ventured downtown, where my uncle Vic owned a barbershop. As a young man, Uncle Vic had erred by copping a neighbor's lawn mower. Since then, he had just menaced society by giving bad haircuts.

A bald man, smelling of lotions and talcum powder, was leaving as I arrived. I made room for this portly client, who was out of breath just from stepping off the barber chair.

"Hey, little Ronnie!" Uncle Vic greeted. He was slapping snipped hair out of a towel.

"Hey, Uncle."

"How's your mommy?" He folded the towel like a flag and set it on the arm of his barber chair.

"She's okay, I guess." Mom was meeting with a friend to peddle Glorietta Cosmetics. But both of them secretly aspired to the next level: Avon.

Uncle Vic slipped a hand deep into his pocket. "Gum?" he offered.

When I nodded, he tore a slice of Juicy Fruit in half and gave me the smaller piece. My uncle had always been cheap, but he could chew your ears with a good story. His talk was free, costing nothing more than the air from his lungs.

I took the gum, unwrapped its silvery foil, and slipped it into my mouth.

"Uncle," I started. "I'm looking for this girl."

"What a little Romeo," he said. "Is she good-looking?"

"Yes, but the girl's for Joey, not me." I refrained

from recounting the rafters incident. Instead, I asked if he had any customers whose daughters were gymnasts.

Uncle Vic raised his face toward the ceiling, exposing a large hairy mole under his chin, a mole that used to scare me when I was little because I thought it was a bloated tick. He snapped his fingers. "There's this guy I used to know. His daughter was into gymnastics. He does air-conditioning now, but when I knew him he was a landscape architect." He laughed and pounded the arm of his barber chair. "Fancy name for a gardener."

I wondered if this was the person Uncle had stolen the lawn mower from, but I didn't have to wonder long.

"I got snagged taking his lawn mower," Uncle Vic volunteered, not in the least embarrassed. "But you know, I wasn't stealing, just borrowing it. I had a girlfriend at the time and I had promised to cut her lawn. You know what I mean?"

I nodded. Uncle had done a stupid thing to impress a girl—just like Joey.

"So where does this air-conditioning guy live?" I asked.

He raised his hand to his mouth and began to massage it thoughtfully. His eyes got bright as he snapped his fingers at me again. "He lives off of Peach Street."

Peach Street was on the edge of town, where people kept chickens, horses, rabbits, and mules. Even pigs were okay if the neighbors didn't complain about the stink and late-night snuffling.

Before I left Uncle Vic cropped my hair for free—or sort of free. I had to sweep the front of his barbershop and scrape up the gum that dotted the sidewalk. Finished, I skateboarded to Peach and Vine, the cool air blowing around my deforested head.

The road was sort of country with the scent of cut grass in the air and the occasional stink of barn animals. Two dusty dogs lay by the road like roadkill. I was sickened. Why hadn't the owners buried them? Then, to my surprise, they flopped from one side to the other. They were just lazy hounds basking in the sun. One raised his head, displayed bloodshot eyes, rolled its loopy tongue around its jaw, and put its head back down.

"Who you lookin' for?" a voice growled.

I spun around, startled. A man on one knee, with a hammer in his hand, was doing something to a gate that was off its hinges.

"I'm looking for this girl," I answered.

The man rose slowly, hooked the hammer on the fence, and studied me.

"What girl is this, boy?" he asked.

His face was rough. A silky scar hung near his mouth, as if he were a fish that had bitten a lure. Age lines wiggled across his brow.

"She's, like, really good at gymnastics," I answered. "Her name's Jessica."

"And why do you want her?"

I plunged ahead and recounted how Joey had climbed up the rafters of the Lincoln High School gym to rescue her balloon.

"Boy, that sounds like a fishy story."

"But it's true." I crossed my heart—twice. I added details about how Coach Bear had bawled Joey out for risking not only his own life but the lives of the people he could have flattened.

A chicken, dusty and fat as a soccer ball, pecked the ground.

"You want to buy a chicken?" the man asked. "Two dollars a pound. She's 'bout three pounds. Six dollars the way she is, or seven if you want her plucked."

He began to plow dirt from under a fingernail with a matchstick. The chicken gazed up, seemingly curious about my decision.

"Nah, sir," I declined. "I'm a vegetarian." I returned to my mission and asked him again if he knew a gymnast.

The stranger pointed. "A girl that used to do flips and stuff lived over there. But she moved." He related a story about how she could fit herself into a cardboard box that was no bigger than a small suitcase. "I don't know how she did it. She was little then, but still." He shook his head and said, "When I looked in that box, she was all folded up. Just one eye was looking at me." He then nudged the chicken back into his yard, but not before trying again to close the sale.

"I'll throw in the plucking for free if you want." He pointed vaguely at a hatchet leaning against the fence.

I shook my head, and the chicken let out a happy cluck.

Chapter 4

I rolled away with no chicken under my arm and only a hint of where Jessica—if it was her—had moved. The man had pointed, saying "Yonder." I was baffled by "yonder." Had I missed this calculation of distance in math class? I also debated the fate of that poor chicken. She was already so fat that her feathers had separated and you could see the skin underneath. It was Saturday. Would she find herself in a stewpot on Sunday?

The country roads quickly led to our town's best neighborhood: The Heights. The expansive lawns were deep green, almost bluish. There were spring colors in window boxes and rows of daffodils in flower beds. In the eaves, wind chimes rocked but hardly made any music.

Three blocks later I encountered my mom at a corner. She was staring at something round and shiny in her hand. At first I thought it was a compass. Was Mom lost?

"Hey, Mom," I yelled. Without a doubt, she'd been out hawking her Glorietta Cosmetics in the better part of Pinkerton. Her briefcase sat at her feet.

"What are you doing here?" Mom asked. She eyed my haircut. "Did your uncle cut your hair, or did Joey?" Joey occasionally mowed my head with a pair of kindergarten scissors, and sometimes I did my magic on his hair.

"Uncle," I answered.

Mom turned my head this way and that, and judged that Joey was the better barber.

"What do you have in your hand?" I asked.

She held up a Sacagawea dollar, which winked a single sparkle, then popped open her briefcase and let me view her loot of fifty-nine more. She had made a hefty sale to a woman who had paid in dollar coins. Mom complained that her back was stiff from lugging the briefcase.

"I'll take them home for you."

Mom brightened at my suggestion. She poured thirty coins into my right pocket and twenty-nine into my left pocket, then gave me one to spend on a soda.

"Go straight home, Ronnie," she told me. I

parted company with Mom and took off on my skateboard, slowing now and then to hitch up my pants. The coins were weighty, and I wasn't sporting a belt to keep my pants up. Each time I propelled myself on my skateboard, I sounded like a tambourine. The coins were like music.

I was two blocks from home when I met Cory, who was sitting on a fence with two of his friends. He unleashed terrible threats, flicked a bottle cap at me, and ordered me to stop or else.

"Come here, monkey face!" he growled. "I wanna talk to you!"

I knew he wanted to pour nasty words into my ears since Joey wasn't with me. However, he was scared that neighbors might hear—an old lady was raking leaves nearby and Cory knew better than to let loose with cusswords. Peppered with age, she was probably hard of hearing, but I suspected that Cory wouldn't chance it.

"I have to go," I hollered in return. I pulled off, my skateboard chipping up sparks against the cement, but Cory and his friends were on my tail.

"Joey," I whimpered. I envisioned Joey pinning Cory in six seconds and doing it again for the fun of it.

"Your friend's not going to help you now!" Cory yelled.

Breathing hard, Cory described how he was going to get me into a headlock, run my nose into the ground, and twist my ears off. The ears he was going to feed to his 4-H project—a hog named Porky.

With the Sacagawea coins jingling in my pockets, I had to hold them down with the flat of my palm. If they spilled, Cory and his friends would jump for them. How could I face Mom, who was walking around the rich part of town in worn shoes? When she wasn't selling cosmetics, she worked at a grocery store, and with Dad gone, every dollar mattered.

I made it home, but my pants almost didn't, as they slid around my ankles when I rounded the corner onto my block. It was this calamity, perhaps, that saved me from a showdown with Cory. He stopped to bend over and laugh, then gave up the chase. But it was no laughing matter.

I took the key from under our front mat and entered the house, my face shiny with sweat. I got a drink of water and noticed that the answering machine's red eye was blinking. I pushed the Replay button.

"Ronnie, can you come over?" The voice was Joey's. I picked up the sound of wind and a bird's chirping. I assumed that his mother had passed her cell phone to him up in the tree. His mother was a super nice mom who let you rob the fruit bowl of all the bananas and apples when you came over.

Joey's voice wasn't edged with urgency. "Come by when you have a chance," he said.

I took a break from my search for Jessica.

For lunch I devoured two quesadillas while I sat on my mom's recliner watching *Animal Planet*. The show was a repeat about an injured female bald eagle rescued from its twiggy nest by a biologist. The first time I caught that episode I had clung to the arm of the recliner, muttering, "Don't let the eggs fall." I pushed my knuckle into my mouth and wept when the biologist discovered that two of the three bald eagle eggs were cracked.

When the program was over, I ventured into the bedroom for a belt. I'd cleared my pockets of the coins, but there was no telling if I might run into Mom again with an additional horde of Sacagawea dollars. I then got a call from this kid named Wilson who wanted to borrow my skateboard. Wilson was freckled, smaller than me, and smarter than most everyone. I said, "Sure," and hid the skateboard under a blanket on the front porch for Wilson to come pick up.

I would have to continue my quest on my bike. I decided to travel a mile to downtown before I went to see Joey. I remembered a ballet school on Main Street that also offered gymnastics classes. First, though, I rode over to Rankle's Drugstore to spend my dollar coin. I pulled a soda from a tub of icy water and approached the front counter.

"What's this?" Mr. Rankle mumbled. Pigeon-chested, turkey-necked, and bird-eyed, he lowered his reading glasses, which had been propped on his forehead. He studied the coin and uttered a grouchy complaint: "I hate these coins."

But he didn't hate it enough to throw it over his shoulder or press it back into my palm. He was a merchant, and money was money. He pocketed the coin and gave me the change—a nickel and a dirty penny.

"I heard 'bout your friend going crazy."

I blinked. I was surprised that even he had heard about Joey's ascent into the rafters.

"You did?" I responded.

"I don't know why he would do that."

I nearly rolled out the story of Joey's first love, but Mr. Rankle was a stingy old man who wouldn't understand. I twisted open the soda and chugged with great reverence, breathing hard as I came up for air. I was about to leave when I spotted a bin of used books for sale—*So Now You're a Teenager* by Justin F. Lockerbie, Ph.D., caught my eye. The cover featured a black-and-white photo of a happy-looking teenage boy and girl walking side by side, hands almost touching. I sneaked a glance at Mr. Rankle and opened the book. It gave off a musty scent as I paused on a page that featured a photograph of a boy, aged thirteen, with splayed ears and Braille-like pimples on his forehead. I swallowed. He reminded me of me, except his eyes were set close, like a rat's. The book was so old, the boy had to be an elderly man by now, or possibly dead and in his grave. I had to wonder whether he ever found love.

"He's a chimp," I unhappily concluded.

I scanned the table of contents as I swigged my soda—the fizz burned my nostrils. Dealing with parents. Containing your anger. Growth spurts, hygiene, and home remedies for pimples. Bullies— Cory popped to my mind. The opposite sex. I chugged long and hard on my soda and was getting comfy to read this chapter when one of Mom's Glorietta Cosmetics customers came into the drugstore. She had a pug nose, tweaked to smell gossip. In fact, she sniffed me out even though I was half hidden behind a beam.

"Hi, Ronnie," Mrs. Fuller greeted smoothly. "I drove by your friend Joey's house. I didn't stop but people are saying that he's living in a tree." She chuckled. "He's acting like a monkey if you ask me. You know anything about it?"

"Uh, no, Mrs. Fuller," I claimed.

"Heard he climbed to the gymnasium roof last night at the awards banquet. Good thing no one was hurt." She licked her thin lips and her pug nose pulsated as she waited for me to offer my impression of last night.

"Yeah, he sort of did that."

Mrs. Fuller waited for more explanation.

"He just, kind of like, you know, got this balloon that went up into the rafters." I lubed my throat with a quick swallow of soda.

"You're sure growing," she remarked and looked me up and down. "What grade are you?"

"Seventh," I answered, and slowly edged away from the book bin. I could see her eyes lower, scan the bin, and lock onto *So Now You're a Teenager.*

"You are a growing boy!" There was a twinkle in her eyes.

"Sorry, Mrs. Fuller, but I have to leave."

"Where are you going? What's the hurry?"

"I have an eye appointment," I lied.

I scooted out in a hurry, the bell on the door ringing that I had lost that round with Mrs. Fuller. I imagined her opening that book on teenagers and maybe pondering—briefly—her own teenage years in ancient times. Try as I might, I couldn't imagine her as a young person. She seemed to have been born an old gossip.

I was glad to escape. As I stepped into the day-light—the noontime sun was knife shiny—I was forced to pleat my brow, narrowing my eyes, in order to see. But I wasn't so blinded that I missed Jessica. She was standing in front of the ballet studio, her hair tied back into a ponytail and a black and pink canvas bag over her shoulder. Her face was as pink as it had been last night.

In a frenzy, I unlocked my bike, tossing the last of my soda away. Most of it sloshed in my stomach as I bent over to pull the chain through the spokes. I had to catch up; Jessica was already climbing into an idling station wagon.

I did a wheelie and headed up the street, grip-ping the handlebars, my mouth clamped closed with determination. The station wagon, I noticed, had a church sticker on the back bumper. The car was headed north. If I lost sight of it, at least I had a clue that Jessica lived in that direction.

I put my sugar rush from the soda to work. My

legs were like pinwheels, and my mouth opened wide and scooped air into my lungs.

"I got to catch her," I told myself.

I was keeping pace when a police car pulled up next to me. I kept churning my legs and gave only a glance to the vehicle. I believe this was my undoing—that single glance and, thus, a sign of disrespect for the law—because a tinted window rolled down. The officer ordered me to stop.

"Who, me?" I yelled, inhaling road dust and car exhaust. I had never been in trouble with the law, though when I was nine I had sweated with worry when Joey and I wrote our names in wet cement.

The officer nodded. I slowed my bike to a halt, dripping from my fiery effort to keep up with the station wagon. My chest was heaving for air.

"Come around over here," the police officer commanded. It was my classmate Madison Keenan's dad.

I rolled my bike to the driver's side.

"What is it, sir?" I asked with exaggerated politeness. My knees were weak, and sweat was beginning to roll off my face.

"You ever see the back of a squad car?" he asked.

I shaded my eyes and stared into the back of the car.

"Don't be a wise guy," the officer grumbled.

"But you said." Then I caught on that he meant *me* in the back of a squad car.

I quickly learned my infraction—littering. Officer Keenan had been parked across the street from the drugstore when I ditched the soda bottle.

"I'll go pick it up," I said and pledged never to litter again as long as I lived. I even offered to pick up litter for a day. If only he would let me go so I could try to catch the station wagon!

But the officer changed the subject and asked about Joey.

"Heard he climbed into the gym rafters last night. Takes a lot of courage to do that. Wonder why he did it."

I searched Officer Keenan's eyes, which were the lightest blue. I wasn't sure what was behind those eyes and was reluctant to respond. Was he really interested in Joey's courage or was he just stalling before he arrested me for littering? I pictured myself in the backseat of the squad car and decided to answer honestly. "This girl lost her balloon and he had to climb way up there to get it." The squad car's engine noise covered up the sound of my nervous heartbeats.

"Do you know if he's going out for basketball when he gets to high school? We could sure use someone who can leap."

"I don't know. That's two years away." I swallowed and tasted dust, car exhaust, and fear. I ventured an answer that might make him happy. "He did mention that he likes basketball."

"We could sure use an athlete like him."

"Joey *really* likes basketball." I feared my nose would grow a couple of feet from this lie.

Officer Keenan put on his shades. "You better not litter anymore," he warned me, and put the squad car into drive. I caught sight of his grin in the mirror, a smile that was almost devilish, before he punched the gas pedal and the back tires screeched up a dust storm.

"He did that on purpose," I spat. I thought I heard laughter from his squad car, but maybe it was the squawk of his radio. The dust the car had stirred up was like a tornado—and inside this funnel stood a teenage chimp.

Chapter 5

The station wagon was long gone. I postponed my search for Jessica, turned my bike around, and sailed on the wave of what I must brag was an awesome wheelie. I set course for Joey's house. I found him still in the tree, and, around the tree, a dozen or so banana skins, apple cores, and the top of a pineapple. Ants were making a holiday of this debris.

"Joey!" I bellowed.

Joey peered down from among the leaves.

"Where you been?" he asked. He pulled a pair of earbuds from his ears.

I struggled up into the tree's lower branches and then made an easy ascent into the higher limbs. I refrained from reporting my detective work in search of Jessica. I didn't want to disappoint my best friend if I couldn't find her. I opted, instead, to tell him about Officer Keenan's interest in him going out for basketball.

"But I don't like basketball." The music from the earbuds whined. I recognized the song by a band called the Gnats.

"But Officer Keenan heard about your climbing way up into the rafters." I gave Joey time to ponder how the story had spread so quickly. I already knew—there were nearly a hundred people at the awards banquet and each was the owner of a tongue, some looser than others.

"People talk," Joey answered. He thumbed his iPod off and the gnatlike sounds ceased.

I had to agree.

"Plus Mom had some friends over for lunch. They came over and looked at me, like I was..."

Like you were a monkey, I nearly blurted.

"Everyone knows," Joey remarked.

We sat in silence. A breeze rustled the leaves. A faraway wind chime made music. After a brief moment of quiet reflection, Joey told me that his mother had baked him banana bread. He asked me if I wanted a slice.

"A delicious thought," I answered. I ate two slices while I mustered up a plan to get Joey out of his funk. "Let's go camping," I suggested. "We take an inner tube down French Creek and try to get really lost. Then we can see if we can get back."

"I'm never coming down. Coach Bear called me a monkey in front of everyone."

"He was just mad. Maybe he would've lost his job if you fell." A thought percolated in my mind. I should find out where Coach Bear lived and ask him to apologize. He would have to do it once he realized Joey was serious about staying in the tree.

"I don't care. He shouldn't have talked to me like that."

Joey had been blasted with insults in front of a girl he liked and with lots of other people around. Any teenage chimp would have buckled under that kind of barrage, but he couldn't stay in the tree forever. I was going to tell him to get over it when his mom's cell phone, near us on a branch, began to ring.

Joey answered. I could hear his mom asking if we wanted lemonade. I licked my lips. I was thirsty from all my running around, as well as hungry. My stomach juices had already pulverized those two lunchtime quesadillas and were working on the banana bread. I assumed that it was only two o'clock or so. Dinner wouldn't be for at least four more hours.

Mrs. Rios delivered the two water bottles filled

with icy lemonade and asked me to remind my mom to visit her.

"I will, Mrs. Rios. And your banana bread was really good." I rubbed my tummy in satisfaction. After she departed, I drank my lemonade in one long stretch.

"Joey," I said softly.

Joey raised his face to me. I could see that two new pimples on his forehead had replaced the dried-up ones on his chin.

"There's this book I saw at Rankle's." I hesitated.

"What about it?" Joey inquired.

"It's called *So Now You're a Teenager.*" I explained what I believed was its thesis, that boy chimps like us in time grow up to be handsome and productive citizens.

"We're always going to be like this!" Joey snapped. "This is permanent. Just look in the mirror!"

"But we might change." I tapped my left knee to illustrate a point. "Our legs are short right now, but I think they're going to grow. Then our arms won't drag on the ground anymore."

"And our ears will magically fold back?" Joey asked snidely.

"Yeah—it could happen." I remembered Mom telling me that life is a continual change—we are babies with no teeth, then babies with teeth, then kids, then teenagers with acne, and then adults whose hair and teeth fall out.

Joey pondered my argument. He peeled a piece of bark and flicked it to the ground.

"Life is about change," I remarked.

"Maybe," he muttered.

My best friend had a great mom and a good dad. His grades were above average, higher than mine, and he could wrestle anyone. Wasn't life good? So what if a few pimples dotted his face? I sighed. Joey was in love, and his dream girl was somewhere in our little town doing cartwheels, backflips, and other daring exercises.

Then an image of Coach Bear played on the screen in the back of my mind. I had to hunt him down and get him to apologize.

"I got to go," I announced abruptly. I dropped like a cat to the ground, landing on my feet.

"Eat and run—is that it?" Joey asked. He feigned anger, but I could see that he was fitting his earbuds back into his ears. I wasn't concerned that he would wallow in loneliness; he had the Gnats to listen to.

"I got to do something," I called up to him. "I'll be back."

I jumped on my bike and returned to the barbershop to ask Uncle Vic if he knew where Coach Bear lived. However, I found my uncle asleep in his barber chair. His mouth was open and a rattling sound issued from its dark cavern. I tiptoed to a chair in the corner. I was determined not to disturb my uncle's departure to dreamland.

To kill time as I waited for him to wake up, I picked up the community newspaper and, to my surprise, discovered that a reporter had covered last night's awards banquet. There was a photo of two awardees—and me, next to them!

"I'll call him," I whispered. The writer was named Gerry Young and his telephone number was listed in the paper. I got up and, like a sneak, used the telephone hanging in the hallway that led to the restroom. It was the heavy black rotary dial kind that maybe some old president might have used in the 1950s.

"Young," a voice announced.

I stalled.

"Who is this?" There was annoyance in his voice. "Is this you, Jason?"

"No, it's me, Ronnie Gonzalez," I answered. "I was at the awards banquet last night."

"What's this about?"

I told him that my best friend was the boy who had climbed into the rafters last night.

"Tell him I want to talk to him!" Mr. Young demanded. His son Jason's baseball team, he said, needed a good center fielder, and though he didn't know if Joey could catch a ball, he had been impressed by Joey's athleticism.

"I guess I can," I said. I then advanced my question. "Do you know where Coach Bear—I mean, Mr. Puddlefield—lives?"

"Why?"

"I have something to return to him."

"How old are you?"

I swallowed and answered, "Forty."

Mr. Young laughed and said, "Stop monkeying around. If you were forty you'd be out playing golf or fishing. That's where Puddlefield is every Saturday."

I paused before I asked, "Which is it, sir? Golf or fishing?" I felt my palms moisten with sweat.

"Fishing, I'd guess. And about your friend—what's his name—tell him to call me. The season's just started. We're only two games out of first."

I risked another question.

"Where's he fishing, Mr. Young?"

Usually at French Creek, he informed me, and was promising to buy Joey a pair of cleats and the uniform, if need be, when I hung up.

I started a tiptoeing trek out of the barbershop when my uncle's eyes peeled open briefly. The eyes closed again, and I got out of there, closing the door carefully. My uncle needed rest from plowing the heads of the men and boys of Pinkerton.

Outside town flows a creek where teenagers gather to stare at the water and sometimes fight, hurl rocks at feral cats, and string cusswords together in new ways. Joey and I didn't fight, or cuss, or consider it our place to hurt the animal kingdom. But we occasionally hauled our loneliness to the creek.

"We're ugly," I recalled Joey lamenting one day when the sky was gray as cement. A depressing fog had settled into the valley.

"How ugly?" I asked.

We were seated on the creek's bank, tossing pebbles into the gray water, where ugly fish showed their faces now and then. Frogs croaked in the reeds and once or twice they revealed themselves—dang, they were way ugly, too. We ate powdery white doughnuts and swigged sodas, a luxury because most of the time we were too broke to splurge like that.

"I don't know how ugly. We just are."

That was two weeks before we turned thirteen and became chimpanzees. In the bathroom mirror, we faced the splayed ears, the flat nose, the bristles of hair on our chins, the arms hanging like garden hoses from our shoulders, and the short, short legs. There was also the side-to-side gait. Why couldn't we have straight noses and long legs like our classmates? Was life cruel, or what?

Now I searched the creek for Coach Bear, the sun flickering behind the leaves of tall eucalyptus. I passed two boys I knew from school—they were hunched like vultures on a downed tree—and grew silent as a cat when I heard Cory's voice somewhere nearby. He was bragging about sighting a dead dog three weeks ago. Cory said that the dog must be really messed up by now.

My heart thumped. Sweat clung to the new growth of hair on my upper lip. I wiped the sweat away and scampered up the creek, freezing to a standstill whenever I thought I heard Cory's voice.

Farther up the creek bank, I found Coach Bear sitting in a small chair, like a king on a dinky throne. He was wearing a hat adorned with a lot of colorful fishing lures, hooks, and a San Francisco Giants button. He was staring sadly at the current's slow chug.

"Something's bugging Coach," I muttered.

"Coach," I called as I high-stepped through the weeds. The dull gaze he presented to the slowly moving current was the same one I recognized on Joey's face.

"Coach Puddlefield!" I waved.

Coach Bear turned his attention to me and blinked.

He called, "Rios."

"Nah, Coach. Gonzalez. Rios is Joey."

Coach Bear's mouth flattened to a line. Maybe he was still angry.

"What are you doing here?" he asked.

"I was just walking by." I sneaked a peek at the fish in his red plastic bucket. Two were smallish and one was so big he was poking out. His head was above the water and his gills were pulsating desperately. I lifted the big fellow out of the bucket and turned him the other way. His face was pointed down so he could breathe—funny how we would die if our faces were *in* water and fish would die if their faces were *out* of water and breathing air.

I got to the point.

"Coach," I started, "I was looking for you. I'm here because you hurt Joey's feelings."

Coach Bear blinked his puffy eyes.

"You see," I continued. "You see, he fell in love with a girl last night, you know, the one who got the gymnastics award." I threw my hands up as I dramatically played out Joey's heroism of retrieving the balloon from way above. Here, I craned my neck skyward until it hurt.

"He's in love?" Coach Bear mumbled. "What does he know about love?"

I hesitated. Yeah, what did Joey know about love? Probably a lot because he had more books than me and once had a pen-pal relationship with a girl from Iceland. So I answered, "Plenty, Coach."

Coach Bear grumbled.

"Couldn't you tell? He took it like—" I considered the plight of the fish whose tail was sticking out of the bucket. "Like that guy there, the one you caught. He was hurting all over, but mostly in the heart."

Coach Bear regarded the preposterously giant fish that could feed a family of four, and maybe their cat, too. He sighed and said, "You know, I thought about that after I cleaned up."

"You called him a monkey—and do you know where he is now?" Coach began to ooze guilt in the form of sweaty nervousness.

"In a tree?" Coach Bear squeaked.

"That's right!"

His eyes glazed over with shame. "Yeah, I guess it's my fault."

I offered a description of Joey's condition. He had been up in the tree in front of his house since before dawn and was living mostly on bananas, pineapples, and apples, plus the generosity of his mother who had baked him banana bread and served homemade lemonade.

"See, Coach, you're already married and know what love is." Now, Coach Bear no longer looked to me like a massive king on a small throne but a fat little boy in a short high chair.

"You got it wrong, Gonzalez. I'm not married." He gazed into the bushes across the creek when he made this pronouncement.

I pointed out his wedding band.

"I can't take it off. Finger's too fat." He shrugged and corrected himself by saying he was married, but separated.

I was respectfully silent. I was convinced that Coach Bear was lonely, and—was it possible?—that he, born and raised in Pinkerton, had once nursed his young loneliness on the banks of this same creek, where the myth goes that two lovers once debarked on an inner tube and were never heard from again.

"Coach," I said softly. "Go visit Joey. Before it gets dark." The sun was wheeling west. In four hours the shadows would begin to creep up from nowhere. I gave him the address.

Coach sighed and absently touched his ring. He asked, "You want a fish?"

I chose the giant fish and left Coach casting his lonely eyes on the water. A hundred or so yards upstream, I returned the fish to the creek. I had asked for mercy from Coach, and I had to demonstrate mercy.

I bid good-bye to that granddaddy fish and sneaked away, catlike. Somewhere Cory lurked in the weeds. Nature could be dangerous.

Chapter 6

I returned home to fill up on bananas and apples, plus a heaping bowl of Froot Loops, and to wash my face and comb my hair. I had to get back to finding Jessica, but first I had to clean up. To get rid of the fish smell, I sprayed myself with cologne, a fine mist of sweetness settling around my throat. Since turning thirteen, I had become obsessed with my appearance, not to mention the scent I threw off.

I was gargling a mint-flavored mouthwash when the front door opened and my mom's voice crowed, "Ronnie, are you home?"

I went out to the living room. "Hi, Mom," I greeted with my fresh breath.

"It was a good day. I sold a lot," she announced as she set down her briefcase. She was happy but tired. Stepping out of her pumps, she moved slowly to her recliner, where after dinner she would park herself and spend an evening watching television.

A good son, I moved quickly into the kitchen to start the kettle—Mom was a tea person. Tea and cookies were her reward for hard and occasionally insulting work. How many times had she felt the breeze of slammed doors? Plenty, I think.

I returned to the living room and waved a hand at the Sacagawea coins on the coffee table. They were safe and sound. I asked if she wanted me to polish them.

"No, that's okay. They're pretty the way they are."

"I've been busy today, too," I remarked.

She presented me with a brief smile as she picked up the *TV Guide* resting on the arm of the recliner.

"I've been looking for this girl," I unwisely announced.

The *TV Guide* dropped from Mom's hands. Was that a storm brewing in her eyes?

"You have a girlfriend?" she asked, none too kindly. "You're too young to have a girlfriend. You should be like other boys and still be playing in mud."

"Nah, Mom, not for me. For Joey." I unfolded the story about Joey and Jessica, and how all signs indicated that he was smitten by love.

"It can't be love," Mom responded. She turned

her attention to the television, off at the moment but an object for her eyes to settle on.

"But it is love. You should have seen him hyperventilate." In truth, he had drooled and leaked a tear. Plus, his knees had become so flaccid that his arms—I swear!—momentarily dragged on the gym floor. I was embellishing this love story with a scene of how Jessica had offered Joey a lock of her hair when the kettle began to sing. I hurried to the kitchen, fixed Mom a cup of tea, and arranged three pig cookies on a plate.

"Very nice," she declared when I returned. She seemed to have forgotten the story of my best friend. She excitedly described her five sales and sipped her tea. She gingerly nibbled the feet off the pig cookies.

"That's great, Mom." I tried to share in her happiness.

I grew courageous as I forged a question that I had been wanting to ask my mom since I turned thirteen.

"Mom, do I look like a chimpanzee?"

Mom lowered her teacup to her lap. She asked me to turn my head sideways, which I did. She offered a long *Hmmmm*. She then asked me to rattle my head from side to side. Again, a long *Hmmmm*. I obeyed her orders to jump up and down and to beat my fists against my chest. She pointed to the doorframe and asked me to swing from it. This was a piece of cake because I had years of practice.

"Yes, you are a monkey," she concluded as she brought the cup of tea back to her mouth. A smile sneaked from the corners of her mouth.

"Mom!" I bawled. She was making fun of me.

"But you are my little monkey." She placed the teacup on the floor. She patted her lap and I jumped onto her cushionlike softness. Mom mumbled how I was growing up to become a nice young man, but could I please not use so much cologne? She sneezed and rubbed her nose.

Too big to sit there long, I was soon out of her lap. If Mom watched *Animal Planet,* she would be more knowledgeable about nature. After all these years, she couldn't judge the difference between a monkey and a chimpanzee. But I figured I'd give her a break. Didn't she provide me with bananas and apples on a daily basis? And what about that blender with forty-four speeds she got me for Christmas?

"Oh, I forgot something," she exclaimed with a pig cookie in her mouth. She rifled through her briefcase for her notepad. "I want you to do a delivery for me."

She sent me to the garage for a box of Glorietta sunscreens, her best seller. In summer Pinkerton roasted under a sun that dazed the rich and poor alike, a sun that by summer's end turned all us kids dark as raisins.

The quest for Jessica would have to wait. I found the box without much difficulty, though I had to climb over stuff in the garage, including my old trike.

"Is this it?" I asked Mom when I got back to the living room. She was sitting with her feet in a pan of hot water. Her feet, already big and flat, were magnified by the water. They were way scary.

Mom lowered her reading glasses onto her nose, poked a hand into the box, and pulled out two tubes of sunscreen. She next sent me to her bedroom for two small boxes—Rainy Times Scrub Gel and Forever Young Skin Lotion.

"I want you to deliver this." She read the name scrawled in her tablet. "Her name is Mrs. Puddlefield and lives over on Barton."

"Mrs. Puddlefield? Coach Bear's wife?" I pictured Coach Bear on the edge of the slow-moving creek.

"That's the lady." Mom wiggled her toes in the pan of hot water. I couldn't help but conjure up an image of the fish in Coach Bear's bucket.

I was soon on my bike with a plastic bag of Glorietta Cosmetics swinging from the handlebars. I rode speedily, pumped up on fruit and six fistfuls of Froot Loops. It was late afternoon, almost four. I still had to track down Jessica by dusk, by which time porch lights would come on and moths the size of bats would flutter around them.

I easily found Mrs. Puddlefield's house on Barton Street. The house was nice and yellowy. There were yellow daffodils and a yellow swing where, I assumed, Mr. and Mrs. Puddlefield had rocked away the evenings when they used to be together. I theorized that Coach Bear, a large man, would have tilted the swing his way. Maybe he had even tipped it over on some evenings when the swing really got going.

I knocked on the front door and swallowed nervously as I heard footsteps.

A young woman with yellow hair answered. "Yes?"

"Hi, I'm Ronnie Gonzalez." I explained that I was the son of the woman who sold Glorietta Cosmetics and had a delivery. I held up the plastic bag to make my point.

The young woman's face softened.

"I know who you are." She beamed happily as she accepted the purchase. "Coach Puddlefield's my dad. You're the one who climbed the rafters last night."

I stalled briefly, but confessed without shame that I would never attempt such an athletic feat.

"You sure? I was there with my boyfriend. You look like the boy." She opened the plastic bag and brought her face to it—she sniffed and remarked that the contents smelled nice.

"I'm sure," I maintained. "I'm Ronnie and my friend is Joey. Joey's the one who climbed up there."

Still, Coach Bear's daughter appeared puzzled. She was positive that I was the one who had retrieved the balloon.

Mrs. Puddlefield edged herself into the doorway. I rigged a smile. "My mom told me to deliver you your products."

The daughter pressed the bag into her mother's arms and disappeared when the cell phone in the waistband of her jeans began to sing a melody. I was thinking of getting out of there, as my job was done, when Mrs. Puddlefield, fiddling with a curler on her head, asked, "Can you do something for me?"

"I guess. What?"

"Climb up on the roof."

"Climb up on the roof," I echoed. She, too, held the notion that I was Joey, the boy who could scale dangerous heights and live to tell his story. I didn't take the time to correct her. I would just help her out and be on my way.

Mrs. Puddlefield leaned a ladder against the house and sent me up to the roof, where I was instructed to turn on the water valve to the evaporator cooler. It was an easy task, and provided me a moment to view the tidy street where neighbors were lacing their lawns with crystal-like fertilizers and children were patting beach balls back and forth. In backyards, laundry swung in the breeze, dogs frolicked, and a father was scouring a barbecue grill with an old rag.

"Joey," I called into the wind. I missed my amigo, my buddy. A weekend was wasted all because of his stubbornness. I blamed him for a second, and then realized, no, he's just in love. He can't help it.

But my lament for Joey vanished when I sighted Jessica two houses away. She was in her backyard jumping on a trampoline. She appeared to be waving at me, but it could have just been her hands going up as she went down.

"It's her," I whispered and then screamed, "Jessica, it's me, Joey's friend! Remember?" No response. I turned up the volume: "JESSICA. IT'S ME! JOEY'S FRIEND!" I then had reason to really scream. In my excitement to get Jessica's attention, I stumbled on the pitched roof, slipped onto my rear end, and began to slide, my palms doing their best to slow my perilous ride. I pitched off the roof into the flower bed, putting an end to the lives of three daffodils that had probably felt pretty with their faces full of the afternoon sun.

"Are you okay?" Mrs. Puddlefield asked. She rushed from the porch, unleashing a few curlers from her head. "Are you hurt?"

My palms stung, and my butt hurt. "Nah, I'm okay."

She began to swat dirt from the back of my pants.

"Really, I'm okay," I argued. I bent over and gathered up her curlers, then spilled them into her palms.

"Oh, my," she sobbed. "I wouldn't have had to even ask you to get on the roof if my husband was still with…"

At that moment I realized that my tumble from the roof provided me an opportunity to extend my role as Cupid. Sure, Mr. and Mrs. Puddlefield had been married for years and years and their hides were thick, so my Cupid's arrows might bounce off them. Still, I had to take the risk.

"Mrs. Puddlefield, I saw your husband at the creek."

A curler rolled from her hand.

More risk. "He seemed sort of sad. He was just

sitting in this really small chair and staring at the water."

Another curler rolled from her palm, but, quick me, I caught it. I picked up the other one from the lawn.

"What were you doing there?"

"I was looking for him because—" I hesitated. How could I explain the drama of last night and how Coach Bear, this woman's husband, had belittled Joey? But I licked my lips and divulged the truth. I told how Coach Bear—though I didn't use that name—had gotten mad at Joey for risking his life and the lives of others. Shoot, Joey could have fallen on anyone, just as the innocent victim was slipping a cookie into his mouth.

"What was he doing up there?"

"He fell in love."

"He fell in love," she repeated slowly. "What did he fall in love with that was up on the ceiling?"

"Rafters," I corrected. "He was in the rafters. And he fell in love with Jessica. Your neighbor. You should have seen him."

I described Joey's smitten nature, minus the drooling. "His knees were so weak I thought I would have to hold him up. That's how much he's in love with Jessica."

"You mean the girl who lives over there?" Mrs.

Puddlefield pointed at the house behind her hedge where two sparrows were bickering among the darkness of the thorny leaves.

"Yes, her—the gymnast. She got an award for doing flips or something." I realized I'd better speed up my narrative—Jessica might climb into a car and vanish before I could talk to her again.

"Coach really does miss you," I blurted out.

"How do you know this?"

"I saw it in his face." I put on a brooding demeanor to illustrate his condition, but told her it was far worse.

She prodded a tear from her eye. She admitted that they were separated and it was her fault.

"Maybe his fault, too, but who cares? I know he wants to get back together." I was not savvy about what causes marital breakups, including my own father's final exit. But I had my calling as Cupid. In my mind, I pulled back the largest bow I could imagine and fired an imaginary arrow—my aim wasn't good, but the effect worked. Her heart, it seemed, began to beat a little harder. Her knuckle found its way into her mouth as she gazed at the yellowish lawn.

"Where did you say you saw him?" she finally asked.

"Yonder," I answered. "Yonder at French Creek."

I had done my job as Cupid for Coach Bear, but I wasn't finished. I galloped to Jessica's house, where I scraped the residue of squashed daffodils from the bottoms of my shoes on her front doormat. I was nervous. I sensed the cologne on my neck had worn off and that my chimp smells were wafting off my body. I stared at the doorbell. What would I say? Tell her how much Joey loved her, or begin by asking if she could teach me to do a backflip? In exchange, I could teach her how to climb a roof and fall off without breaking any bones.

"Here goes," I whispered and was raising my wandlike finger to the doorbell when I heard "Hey, orangutan butt!" I turned.

"Who, me?" I asked, pointing a finger at my chest.

"Yeah, you, doofus."

Cory and his two friends were standing on the sidewalk, breathing like rhinos. Their faces were dirty, their hair a forest of grass, leaves, and small twigs.

"We need another person to play football," one of Cory's friends bellowed. "You can be on my team even though you're a wimp."

"But I gotta go do something," I answered earnestly.

"You don't need to do anything," Cory retorted. "And Joey isn't around to help you. Heard he's in a tree and ain't never coming down."

My best friend had assigned himself to a tree for the rest of eternity. How would I get along without him? Would it mean that Cory would return to beating me up daily? Or would force me to play football so he could beat me up on the field?

I lowered my head, full of disappointment, and stumbled down the steps as one of Cory's friends began to drag me to the sidewalk.

"Hurry up, man," he growled. "I gotta be home by six!"

But some good had come out of my jaunt to Mrs. Puddlefield's. Besides learning how to turn on the water valve of an evaporator cooler, I turned on the valve behind Mrs. Puddlefield's eyes—she did sob for a few seconds. I prayed for her reconciliation with Coach. I prayed they would come together in time to eat those two other fish he had snagged from the creek.

But, best of all, I had located Jessica. I would visit her later and plug her with my arrow.

Chapter 7

As the sun dipped behind springtime trees and the blue jays reined in their screeches for the day, I returned home with mud on my knees, elbows, pants, and the previously unblemished territory of my face. Mom smiled as she sized up my filth. She sang with gusto, "Oh, you're still my little boy!" Then she ordered, "Get the vacuum. You're dirty!"

From the closet I pulled out our small round vacuum cleaner, whose unwieldy hose was like the tentacle of an octopus. I submitted to Mom's getting the worst of the dirt off by running the hose around my head, across my chest, over my belly (I laughed as the suction pulled at a layer of my skin), and down to my wiggling toes. Later, when I emptied the paper filter, I was amazed by the amount of dirt that had come off me.

"I'm way hungry," I crowed. I couldn't believe

how much energy it took to be repeatedly tackled by Cory and his friends. But Mom ordered me to shower first.

In the shower I assessed my bruises—three on my legs, four on my arms, and scores more on my back. Cory's friends played pretty rough. They all outweighed me by plenty, and toward the end of our game, I was just too slow to avoid their tackles. I hunched my shoulders, lowered my head, and gritted my teeth. I saw stars of various shapes when our heads bumped. I limped. I rolled on the ground. Cory threatened that if I quit, he was going to deploy a new kind of karate chop only a few special practitioners had mastered. Though only a yellow belt, he threatened to unleash an inner power that could break a coconut. He snarled that my head resembled a coconut and this secret chop of his would do the trick.

So I played.

Now at home, fresh from the shower, I sat down to a comfy meal of macaroni and cheese, a salad with ranch dressing, and—spoiled me—a banana milk shake with a cherry on top. I ate and burped as I scratched my contented belly and rolled my tongue around my mouth. After I was satisfied, I remembered Joey. I pictured him clutching a tree limb, empty of belly, his tongue hanging out for want of drink, maybe weeping, maybe sucking his thumb from loneliness. I pictured a horrific storm climbing over the mountain, the same mountain where sometimes on windy days we were sure we heard the faint musical sounds of people having fun, pleasures that never seemed to reach us folks in Pinkerton.

"Mom," I announced with both hands resting on my belly. "I'm going to go see Joey." I had spent so much time playing Cupid for my best friend that I hadn't made time to actually be with him.

"Did you get enough to eat?" she asked. She didn't look away from the television.

"Mom, Joey's in a tree, and he needs my help."

"Don't worry, I'll do the dishes."

"Mom, you're not listening!" I was now down on my knees at her side.

Mom peeled off her glasses from the bridge of her nose. "Why?" she inquired.

"Because he's in a tree, I told you, and he won't come down."

Mom munched on a fingernail as she mulled over whether to give me permission to venture out in the evening. "And so you want to live in a tree, too? Monkey see, monkey do—is that it?"

"Mom, we're not monkeys," I replied. "We're chimps. Monkeys have tails and chimps are more like people. Don't you know that chimpanzees can type?"

"What do they type, sweetheart?"

"They can type things like *help* and *hungry now.*"

Mom cooed that I was her sweet boy. She teased that when I was still in my Pampers, "Hungry now" had been my favorite phrase.

"Come on, Mom. Can I please go?"

She sighed and gave in. She said that I had to be home by—she peered at the Porky Pig clock on the mantel, a clock that wagged its piggy tail for each second—by nine, nine thirty at the latest.

I departed with my pockets stuffed with two bananas and an apple, a little sustenance for Joey. I was hightailing it on foot when I decided to return to get my bike—I preferred my skateboard but it was now in Wilson's hands. I hurled myself onto my bike, found the pedals, and sped away.

Within three blocks of my house, two older teenagers motioned me over. Their truck was in the middle of the street, stalled, both doors open. Music was coming from the cab, but its twangy country chords left me cold.

"Give us a hand," the one with a doughnut in his hand said in a demanding voice. He bit into the doughnut and most of it disappeared.

I swung a leg off my bike and held on to the handlebars.

"I'm not that strong," I confessed.

"You look strong," he countered after he cleared his throat of doughnut.

At this compliment, I puffed out my chest. After all, I was thirteen and growing in quarter-inch spurts. And when I did sit-ups, didn't my stomach reveal the start of a six-pack? Weren't shadows playing on my biceps when I did chin-ups? And what about the three hairs on my chest?

"What you got in your pocket?" the other teenager asked. His voice, almost girlish, sounded as if he had been inhaling helium.

"Bananas and an apple," I answered, my head hanging. I could see these two smart alecks were ready to pitch laughter into my face.

They only laughed a little. The one who had eaten the doughnut asked, "Are you a monkey?"

Couldn't people get the difference between monkeys and chimpanzees? Plus, why was he so high and mighty? He had the makings of a warthog; tusks were showing from his closed and bulky mouth.

I set my bike at the curb, relinquished the better of the two bananas to the warthog, and got down to business.

"Come on, man, put something into it," the warthog belched. He had positioned himself on the driver's side, and his friend was stationed on the passenger's side. Both seemed to be putting a lot of effort into the task.

At the back of the truck, I gritted my teeth and pushed with all my might. In my belly, the banana shake sloshed and, I guess, was turning into energy.

"Come on—push!"

"I am," I snapped.

The truck picked up speed and came alive when the warthog jumped in and popped the clutch. The other teenager hopped in and the doors slammed like gunshots. They didn't yell "Thanks" or wave a hand from the window. No, the truck coughed smelly black smoke I could see against the street-light. It disappeared, its red back lights full of evil.

Evil—that's the word. When I went to retrieve my bike, it was gone.

"They stole it!" I cried. I was certain that the two teenagers were scam artists. A third friend must have been hiding in the bushes.

I stood defeated in the middle of the street, my arms at my sides, suddenly tired. It had been a long day that started with a blue sky over beautiful daffodils, but now the smell of truck exhaust hung in my nose. *How could they do that to me?* I lamented. *I wouldn't do that to them!*

I had lost my bike, but at least I still had Joey. I

embarked on my legs—trusty getaway sticks—to go get sympathy from him. And as I walked in the gathering dark of Pinkerton, indifferent to barking dogs and the occasional security light going on as I ghosted down quiet streets, I wondered if Joey's tree would one day be a shrine for those seeking love.

To my amazement, Joey was enjoying modern comforts such as a tiny television (presently off and trailing a long extension cord), an ice chest with a thermos of mango juice, a radio (battery operated), a three-speed blender (also battery powered) for smoothies, an air mattress, a kerosene lamp, and a small library of *National Geographics*.

"Wow," I exclaimed.

I had climbed into the tree via a rope ladder and reiterated a second and third "wow" when I spotted a colossal fruit bowl filled with a cornucopia of nature's best. The banana and apple in my pockets seemed a paltry gift; yet, I pulled them out. The banana was so mushy from my fiery strides pushing the truck that I contemplated heaving it and the bruised apple away. But Joey said he would toss them into the blender and whirl them into a smoothie for a nightcap. Here I issued another "wow," and listened to a brief lecture from my friend on waste not, want not.

"It's like home!"

"Yeah, it's nice. I figure if I'm never coming down, at least I should live well."

Joey said his mind would not turn into mush like my banana. He would continue his studies. He opened a laptop computer and its screen glowed like a treasure.

"I could even take college classes later."

"Shut up."

"Yeah, really." He went to a website and a catalog popped up, displaying courses for eager-beaver students who were bored with high school and were searching for a challenge.

"You've got everything." I was bewildered. I had been convinced that Joey was suffering as he wasted away, hugging a limb to keep from falling. But I had been too hasty. "Does that mean you're never coming down?"

"Why should I?" He said this without anger or stubbornness. He pointed to a high crooked branch. "Follow me, Ronnie."

I climbed awkwardly behind him. He was more sprightly than me because he had many hours of practice living in a tree. The two of us tottered on a branch that was skinny but pliable.

"That's Venus," Joey pointed out.

"It is?" I didn't know my planets or stars, though

I did enjoy their twinkly effect and was glad that they kept their distance from Earth. I had heard that if a star just grazed our planet we would flare like matchsticks. I was too young to go up in smoke.

"Over there is Orion and the Big Dipper." He informed me that an astronaut could be shot up in a spaceship going a zillion miles an hour and never reach Orion.

"Really?" I asked.

"Yeah, really. So it's better that we don't try. We would be like really dead by the time we got there."

We returned to the platform and sat cross-legged on pillows. Joey handed me a blanket. I was grateful for its warmth, as it was surprisingly cold in the tree. Joey next explained that the tree was mostly water.

"Shut up!" I crowed.

"Yeah, really! Trees are mostly water because they are thirstier than you think. They pump up gallons and gallons of water daily." Joey acquainted me with more news: we were mostly water, too.

"What about our bones?"

"They're water, too. Well, mostly."

He went on to point out that porcupines, elephants, and even tarantulas were mostly water. I smacked my lips, an unsubtle hint that we should break for a drink. Joey, a good host, poured me a paper cup of mango juice, though I would have pre-ferred hot chocolate. The night was chilly.

"What have you been doing today?" Joey asked.

I licked the sweetness from my lips and offered him a big fat lie, or at least a partial one. "I went down to the creek to look at fish." I was reluctant to bring up Coach Bear's name, or to inform him that I had been scouting for Jessica. One, I wasn't sure my efforts would pan out. Two, I was now relishing a second cup of mango juice, along with a trail mix of crushed almonds and walnuts, unsalted sunflower seeds, and tiny chocolate chips. Three, I judged if I provided a list of my accomplishments—plus fail-ures—it would alter our mood. It was good to see Joey enjoying his new life in the tree.

Then I reported the bad news.

"Someone stole my bike, Joey."

"No!" Joey put down his paper cup and finished chewing a mouthful of his trail mix. "That's messed up."

"Yeah, I was riding over to see you, and these two guys tricked me. Their truck was, like, in the middle of the street, and they needed me to help them push it." I painted a picture of my shoulder pressed to the back of the truck and pushing with all my strength.

"I'm surprised the truck didn't shoot off into space. You got a lot of leg strength."

I eyed Joey. "You mean that?"

"Yeah, Ronnie, you're stronger than you think."

I enjoyed hearing those words and was waiting for him to say more when the truck I helped rounded the corner onto Joey's street. It approached loudly.

"That's the truck!" I stood up, angry and ready to parachute from the tree and run after it.

The truck popped foul exhaust, and from the cab a bottle flew and crashed against the ground. Then a banana peel flew out from the driver's side.

"I gave him that banana," I bawled.

At the stop sign, the truck barely applied its brakes as it rounded the corner. By the glow of a streetlight, I could see my bike in the back. I considered swinging from the tree and running after the truck, but what would have been the use? I was fast, but not Superman.

"I know that truck," Joey announced. Even in the dark, I sensed a hot glow on his cheeks and fire in his eyes.

"Who are those guys?"

"That's Cory's half brother. He's in eleventh grade but my brother used to wrestle him." Joey turned to me. "Are you sure he's the one who stole your bike?"

I nodded. For a long time we stared at the place where the truck had recklessly skidded around the corner and listened for the sounds of the truck's popping exhaust.

I borrowed Joey's mom's cell phone and called Mom to ask if I could sleep over at Joey's. She agreed, but said she wouldn't take me to the hospital if I fell out of the tree and cracked open my head. Of course, this was sort of a joke, and I released a chuckle to suggest that she was a really funny mom. However, I could sense that Mom might be worried about my new status as a tree dweller.

I bedded down next to Joey. For a while we watched the stars slowly wheel westward. Then Joey got up and made that smoothie out of the banana and apple I had brought from home, adding portions of a pineapple and some sort of berry. That sweet brew was history in no time.

Then it was back to bed.

"Joey," I mumbled, near sleep. "Are we going to stay chimps?" I had my fingers crossed that we were just in phase two of our growth as human beings, that in a few months we would wake up and find new faces in our steamy bathroom mirrors. We would wipe the mirrors, and discover we were just regular boys.

"I think so."

"Really?" I had expected a more philosophical answer. I was too tired to worry. I yawned and pulled on the blanket—Joey was a hog when it came to sharing it. I folded my hands behind my head. Through the leaves I followed the flights of occasional airplanes, and had started inventing stories about the people in the planes when a shock ran through me.

I sat up and scratched my head.

"I know what to do," I mumbled. Joey, thumb in his mouth, was asleep. I lay back down as I played out my plan in my mind. It took me only a short while to lower my eyelids and slide down a roof into a happy dream.

Chapter 8

The next morning when I returned home on foot, I found Mom in the kitchen stirring a pot of oatmeal. She seemed nice and toasty in her fleece-lined robe, and her big woolly slippers added to this image.

"How did you sleep?" she asked. She raised a wooden spoon to her mouth, and her tongue, lizard fast, darted out for a taste.

"Pretty good but the birds woke me up," I answered. I would have broken the news about my stolen bike but I didn't want to spoil her breakfast. I poured myself a mug of milk and sat down at the kitchen table, where I took a knife and, in a swashbuckling manner, cut a chunk of coffee cake.

"Mom," I said. "I'm going to church." Last night I had remembered the church bumper sticker on Jessica's car and had a hunch that she would be there that morning.

"You're what?" Mom appeared confused.

"I'm going to church." My mouth churning a piece of coffee cake, I repeated my Sunday morning plans before I dipped another piece of cake into my milk. Crumbs floated on the surface, but there was no escape for them. It would be only a matter of time before I drained the mug.

Mom put the wooden spoon down and shifted her oatmeal to the back burner. She squeezed me affectionately.

"I'm proud of you! My little monkey is going to church all by himself."

"Yeah, Mom, I thought I would try it out." I grabbed a banana from the fruit bowl.

Moved by my apparent holiness, Mom spooned me a bowl of oatmeal and blessed it with a handful of raisins. Then she rushed from the kitchen and returned holding up a Sacagawea dollar.

"Take this for the offering." She dropped the coin into my shirt pocket.

After our breakfast dishes were steaming on the drainboard from a good scrubbing, I looked in the phone book for the name and address of the church. The sticker, I remembered, showed something like a cross with a red scarf. Maybe I could find the symbol in the church's listing in the Yellow Pages. When I did, I saw that Jessica was United

Methodist. I didn't know the church, as our household belonged to St. John's. We seldom went to Mass, which, Mom said, was a sure sign we were Catholic.

I checked the address. "Easy," I whistled. "I know where that is."

The church was downtown. I looked up at the Porky Pig clock on the mantel. It was 9:35.

"I'd better hurry," I muttered.

I would have asked Mom for a ride, but she was sweetly content in her recliner, a blanket around her knees. She was tapping a finger as she waited for the San Francisco Giants, her favorite team, to come on television. They were playing back East.

I dressed in my best clothes, sprayed my throat with cologne, and brushed my teeth until they hurt. While I was slipping into my dress shoes, an idea came to me.

"My trike," I murmured. I realized that I would look absurd—a thirteen-year-old dressed in Sunday clothes riding a trike—but I needed a way to get to church pronto. My skateboard was lent out and my bike was stolen. If I stood up on the pedals I figured I could still get there faster than by walking.

I pulled the old trike from the garage, wiped its seat and handlebars free of dust, and spurted oil on the front and back axles. I swallowed my pride. If I pedaled really fast maybe no one would recognize me. My face will be a blur, I tried to convince myself. People will just think I'm big for my age.

A horde of kids along the way, plunging Popsicles into their stained mouths, recognized me. But what did I care? I was resolved to get to church on time. I guessed it would probably start at ten o'clock, but I was late by ten minutes. I raked the sweat from my brow and upper lip, shook at my shirt to cool my back, and strode into the church. But I braked immediately.

"Uncle!" I cried. Shouting on holy ground was probably bad form. I punished my mouth for its outburst by slapping a hand over it.

"Ronnie," Uncle Vic greeted. He was dressed in a brown suit and white shoes with silver buckles. His socks were orange. His tie was eggplant purple and rippled with wrinkles. I wasn't up on churchy fashions, but it was my feeling that Uncle was dressed weird. I wondered if he was color-blind.

"So this is the church you go to?" I sensed my mouth was hanging open and I closed it. "Mom said you were going someplace different."

"This is it!" He beamed at me and jokingly asked, "Who lowered your ears? Your haircut looks just awful!" Uncle was unaware of my sensitivity about my ears, but he knew who had run barber clippers recklessly around my head.

"It's good to see you!" he cried. He gave me a quick hug and patted my cropped hair. I presumed he was the usher when he held open the door to the sanctuary and gave me a strong push. I entered with my hands in semiprayer; the fingers were laced, but not shaped into a steeple. Music played while I lingered by the back wall for a few minutes. I scanned the members. Almost all the men sported the same kind of haircut that crowned my gourd. Everyone was singing with gusto and scenting the air with breakfast smells. I smelled ham and eggs, and waffles with little weenies on the side. The congregation was well fed, even sort of porky. One woman was so large that many children could stand in her shadow and be cool on a hot day.

The pastor, though, was a skinny man with a skinny tie. His singing voice was weak and his face plain as a piece of toast. But I liked him because he didn't embarrass me by announcing my sudden presence with a loud, "Now, who's this young man?" He just nodded his head in my direction.

I found a seat near the front. I spotted Jessica immediately, for she was at the piano—the girl was multitalented! Her pretty hands were on the ivories, except when she had to spank her sheet music back into place. It kept trying to close as she drummed out a slow song about rocks, flocks, and mighty winds.

The song ended and Jessica stood up, smoothing the back of her dress. She started to take her seat in a pew, but paused when she recognized me, then maneuvered in my direction. As she sat next to me, she smiled.

"My uncle comes here," I confided. I knew I probably shouldn't whisper in church, but I needed to lay the groundwork for our conversation. Everything was going according to plan. I was sure I would have a chance to talk to Jessica after church. She bit and asked, "Who's your uncle?"

"I'll give you a hint. He's a barber."

"Oh, you mean Mr. Mendoza."

I nodded and ran a hand over my head to signify that he had just cut my hair. I then turned my attention to the pastor, who was standing behind the pulpit shuffling papers. His cough was theatrical. He wiped his eyeglasses, also theatrically, before he set them back on his face and began his sermon.

While it didn't last long—ten minutes, the time it took me to eat two Life Savers—I couldn't absorb a word. I was too conscious of Jessica beside me. She was beautiful as a flower—no, lots of flowers set in a vase next to a crystal fruit bowl filled with bananas and apples. I could swear that the blood in me was rushing at super speed. Although when I'd met her at the awards banquet I'd been more interested in the cookies, now I couldn't blame Joey for liking her. She was not only beautiful, but she could do backflips, play the piano, and probably engage her mind in lots of other things. She also smelled good.

I turned to see if I knew anyone else and gulped when I spotted Mrs. Fuller, the gossip. She waved at me and hoisted a smile that was closer to a scowl.

"What's wrong?" Jessica asked.

"Nothing," I answered. My mouth was dry; most of my moisture was now on my face in the form of sweat.

I then nearly jumped when I noticed the two teenage boys who had scammed me and stolen my bike. They were down the row, slouched in the pew with their feet out in the aisle. I saw their dirty tennis shoes with the blackest of shoelaces, which had me musing whether their heartless souls were like that, too. Then a revelation struck me and **moved** the contents of my breakfast in my stomach—it was that strong. Was it possible that we humans were like shoelaces? You can either be tied up properly, or dragged through littered gutters.

Jessica touched my forearm again to point out

that an elderly gent was reaching toward me with a wicker basket.

"Oh, I'm sorry." I produced the Sacagawea dollar from my shirt pocket and dropped it into the basket.

Once again I turned my attention to the two teenagers. They had locked their gaze on me, and it was anything but angelic. I figured if they were there, Cory would be somewhere in the church, too. The warthog mouthed a word in my direction, or was he getting ready to break into song?

Jessica had moved from my side back to the piano. She began to pound out "Rock of Ages." We sang that one and another about storms, and then the pastor descended six carpeted steps from the altar. He asked, "Birthdays! Who's celebrating a May birthday?" I imagined a cake with a hundred candles.

"Come on, don't be shy," the pastor called cheerfully. "Come on, ladies. Boys! Mr. Roskin, I know your birthday's in May."

There was some shuffling in the pews and rattling of church bulletins. Soon six churchgoers of varying ages stood in front—and one was Cory! There he stood in a white shirt, bow tie, and blue blazer. His hair was combed, his face scrubbed, his mouth solemnly closed. His pants rode high, revealing orange socks, which made me think that maybe I missed a fashion phase.

Cory's eyes slid in my direction. He furrowed his brow, confused by my presence. He mouthed a word. What did he want? He formed a complete sentence that was something like *Wait for me.*

I mouthed back, *Why?*

I received no reply because Cory's mother glared at him to knock it off. I was familiar with that kind of motherly look.

The congregation sang "Happy Birthday." The birthday crowd received orange pencils.

"You are older...," the pastor announced with his arms out. One of the women frowned at this exclamation.

"...and wiser," the pastor heralded. "We'll have cake in the basement."

Service broke up like a football huddle, and the yawn that had been building inside me finally materialized. But I was polite enough to hide it behind a hand, and with that yawn-scented hand I shook hands with an elderly gentleman with hearing aids in both ears. He seemed glad to see me.

Before there was a rush to the door, I pulled Jessica aside and asked if I could see her later.

"Why?" she asked.

"It's about Joey, the guy who climbed into the rafters."

Jessica beamed and told me to come by her house around four. She would have to eat Sunday lunch and finish her homework before her mom would let me do anything else. She gave me directions to her house, but I knew already.

My exit from church wasn't a cinch. Jessica left when her mother called her, and then a gloved hand latched onto my arm. The hand belonged to Mrs. Fuller.

"Greetings," she sang. She smelled heavily of perfume.

"Hi," I answered weakly.

"It's good to see you in church."

I gazed around and pronounced, "It's a neat place."

Mrs. Fuller clutched my forearm. Behind a face caked with makeup, she observed that I was such a growing boy. Her eyes locked knowingly on me as I realized she was recalling *So Now You're a Teenager*.

"You know, we have a youth group. You should join."

I imagined the warthog as the leader of the youth group. One of our activities could be going

through people's glove compartments while everyone was in service.

She lowered her face to my ear and asked in a
minty whisper, "How come you were talking to the
Bentley girl? Is there something between you and
her?"

"She's helping me with homework," I lied.

With that revelation, Mrs. Fuller smiled and revealed lipstick on the front row of her sharklike
teeth. She was smelling blood. I think it was my
blood.

"Oh, is that right?" she responded. She waited
for me to tell her more. I tried to get away politely,
but her hand gripped my arm. Dang, she was
strong. Anchored in boxy shoes and with her weight
behind her, she was a mighty force. With her other
hand, she fanned herself with the church bulletin,
circulating her perfume around my face. I recognized the scent. It was called Morning Glory.

"You will come back, won't you?"

"Yeah, I will, but I gotta go now."

Mrs. Fuller frowned. "You mean 'have to go.'"
She proceeded to straighten my tie—I had the funny
sensation she was going to close it like a noose.

"Yes, I have to go," I exclaimed.

"You are a growing boy."

"Yes, but I have to go," I repeated, and got away when Mrs. Fuller snapped open her purse to look for a comb. She said that my hair was standing up wickedly as horns.

I waved to Uncle Vic as I scampered from the church, breathing hard. I expected Cory to be waiting for me, or his half brother and his friend standing at their truck and calling me to get in for a one-way ride to the country. Instead, in the blinding light of a spring day, I found my bike leaning against the lower steps. I rocked on my heels. It was that Sunday I began to believe in miracles.

"You're back," I greeted in song. I ran down to my bike. The chrome handlebars added shine to my miracle.

Chapter 9

I sped away with a halo of sun beaming down on me. I was happy, even blessed, for I did shake the pastor's hand, avoid the warthog and his friend, and donate my trike to the church rummage sale. And I finally spoke face-to-face to Jessica. I'm sure she pondered my purpose between bites of birthday cake in the church basement.

I figured that I had five hours before I would meet up with her. What should I do? I didn't want to see Joey because my mission wasn't accomplished yet. I worried that if I returned home, Mom would put me to work digging up weeds in the flower bed. Or she might assign me to wash the windows clean of winter's shadowy dirt. Or maybe take a broom and get the spiderwebs off our dead extra car in the driveway—Dad had sold the engine before he took off with that woman in a sports car.

I rode aimlessly until my curiosity drew me to a yard sale. A man in overalls sat on an overturned bucket surrounded by stuff that he had dragged from his garage. He rose on his gimpy legs when he saw me coming. He ran a hand over his whiskery jaw. A transistor radio in the front pocket of his overalls was tuned to the Giants baseball game.

Most of his merchandise was pots and pans, large print *Reader's Digest*s, a coffeepot, a child's guitar with no strings, old sleeping bags, and dresses as spacious as tents. The dresses, I supposed, belonged to his wife.

"Can you use a set of screwdrivers?" he asked.

I told him no.

"How 'bout a birdcage?" He informed me that his wife had been fond of canaries. He kicked the grass and stated, "She's gone."

I guessed that his wife had passed away. I could have asked when or how, but it was none of my business. Her dresses were on the lawn and twelve or so pairs of shoes were parked in a line.

"Nah, not really, sir."

"Birds make nice pets. When you talk to them, they sing back. I'll throw in the birdseed."

Still, I deflected his efforts to sell me a birdcage and his insistence that a pair of rusty roller skates would build up my legs and bring me hours of hap-

piness. He tried to convince me that a cookie jar
would be an ideal gift for Mother's Day and that a
battery-operated handheld personal fan would be a
dream come true for my father.

"I'm just looking, sir," I confessed to the man,
who then said, "Hey, then, how about if you help
me." He pointed toward his roof. "I got to turn on
the water valve on my cooler. Too old to get up
there."

My last trip up a roof had brought me bruises
and dark memories of crushed daffodils. I shaded
my eyes as I took a step back to view the roof's
pitch. It didn't look so steep, and the old guy
needed help.

"You got a ladder, sir?"

"No, but I can boost you up from the back of
the house."

"How will I get down?"

The man posted his meaty hands on his hips.
"Why, you jump. You're young. Like a kitty cat, you
got nine lives in you."

I was tempted to alert him that I had used up
one of my lives yesterday at Coach Bear's house,
and that at this rate I would be dead by the following weekend.

"But I have my church clothes on," I countered.
Certainly, even if he was as old as the oldest hills, he

could envision a mother's anger if her son dirtied his best clothes. It might even make her suspicious about whether he had actually been to church or gone to some pigpen with his buddies.

"Hmmm, you do have some nice duds on." The gentleman suggested that I wear one of his wife's dresses over my good clothes. I balked.

"Come on, it's just for a few minutes. Shoot, I wear her slippers," he boomed. "And they're pink!"

Thus, with a pair of pliers in my back pocket and a long dress flapping around my ankles, I clambered onto a roof at the height of treetops and TV antennas. I stood up with my hands out for balance and walked up the sloped roof, the asphalt shingles crumbling under my steps. I reached the boxy cooler and ripped off the black plastic covering that protected it during winter. I opened one side and tried to turn the valve with my fingers. No luck. Then I let the pliers bite down on that stubborn little valve. I gave it a half turn and water immediately sang in the copper tubing.

Finished with my task, I took in a view of Pinkerton. I liked our town, and I liked my friend, Joey, who I feared would never come down from the tree.

"Hey, Joey," I called, though my amigo was far out of hearing range. "Joey, Joey, Joey!"

At that height, I felt the wind in my hair and a mighty stirring in my soul. Splayed ears and all, I was glad to be alive. Joey and I had been friends since we were in Pampers, and we would be friends when we were old men and once again in Pampers.

I felt a jerky motion under my feet. "What the heck!" I yelled. My body jerked once more, as if some joker had pulled a rug out from under me. I righted myself. Then I realized the shingles were crumbling under my shoes, then shifting loose. My arms went up, waving for balance. Momentum built as I began to surf off the roof.

"Like, yikes!" I sped toward the edge of the roof, my tender life passing before my eyes. I saw bowl after bowl of cereal laden with sliced bananas whizzing past. I saw strawberries in cream. I saw candy apples, quesadillas, vegetarian soups, slices of cheese pizza, pretzels large as horseshoes. I saw my mom at the blender fixing an afternoon smoothie and toast popping up from a chrome toaster. Had my life consisted of nothing more than food?

Upright and waving, I dismounted the roof, landing on my feet like a cat.

"Now, that didn't hurt," the old gentleman said. "Boy, at your age you can fall from the Empire State Building and just get up and dust yourself off."

My legs buzzed, the soles of my feet stung. But

I did seem unhurt, though my hands felt just a fraction of an inch closer to the ground. Had my spine collapsed a bit?

"Did you turn the valve on?" the man asked.

I nodded as I shrugged out of the dress and handed the pliers back to him. I took a slow Frankenstein step, then another cautious step. My lower half seemed to function quite nicely, and the upper half obeyed the orders from central command in my brain.

"I got a little something for you."

"What?" I asked.

When the gentleman flipped a coin in my direction, I caught it in midair. A Sacagawea dollar.

"Thanks, sir," I chimed.

I was feeling pretty religious at the moment. Hadn't I just given up such a coin at church, and now another had come my way? *Wow,* I thought. I straddled my bike, located the pedals, and pushed off, richer by a coin. I had used two of my lives jumping from roofs. Seven more to go.

I imagined Joey in the tree juggling apples and oranges, and imagined one of the apples slipping from his grip. I should be there to retrieve that slippery fruit. But I decided to stay away—for now. And with a few hours to kill, I couldn't go home or Mom would put me to work. I couldn't go to the playground for fear that I would run into Cory. I was nervous about why he had wanted me to wait for him after church, and might be mad that I hadn't. I decided to splurge on a soda and a bag of sunflower seeds. I could take my treat to the courthouse and sit in the shade of one of the old oak trees, watching old men play dominoes. With my Sacagawea coin and a few other dimes and nickels in my pocket, I was worth something.

I was in the refrigerated section of the market when I spotted Coach Bear. He saw me as he let the fogged glass door close.

"Hi, Coach." I approached him, not really happy about this encounter, but seeing no way to escape. I had learned details about his personal life and his separation from his wife. I had witnessed his tantrum at the gym. I wondered if my face gave away my embarrassment.

"Is Joey still in the tree?" He was gripping a jar of tartar sauce.

I told him, yes, he was still in the tree.

Coach Bear sighed and dropped the tartar sauce into his basket.

"You know, I think I was too rough on him," he admitted.

My silence indicated that I agreed. It was clear

that Coach hadn't gone to see Joey yesterday, but maybe he still would.

"Coach," I started, "I delivered some cosmetics to your wife. My mom sells the stuff." I was mindful that he was a bearish man with thick fur, and maybe my Cupid's arrow wouldn't pierce him. Still, in my mind's eye, I pulled back my bow and aimed one at him.

He stopped in his tracks and touched his heart. "You did?" he responded in a shaky voice. "She said some boy came over yesterday."

"That was me." I swallowed a sour gob of fear and braved, "You have a nice wife."

"*Did* have, you mean."

"Nah, Coach, she's still your wife."

Coach Bear looked down at his basket of food. There were a couple of lemons, parsley, asparagus, lettuce, ranch dressing, vanilla ice cream, and the tartar sauce.

"I'm having dinner with her."

"You are!" I cried gleefully. I imagined them seated together, Coach Bear's elbows up on the small table.

"She doesn't know it yet, but I'm gonna cook for her." He gazed in the direction of a soft drink sign shouting in loud letters TWO FOR ONE.

"What are you gonna cook?"

"Remember those fish?"

"You know how to cook fish?" I asked.

"Yeah, you gut them, which I already took care of yesterday, and fry them in a pan with hot oil." He described his secret flavoring and the side dishes of asparagus and a green salad with croutons.

"I gotta go," he said and proceeded toward the checkout.

"I gotta go, too." Mrs. Fuller and her insistence on correct grammar came to mind. I could even smell her perfume and feel that powerful grip on my forearm. I let that image recede, like bathwater down a drain.

I trailed Coach Bear to the cashier, where he took my soda and sunflower seeds from me. "Let me pay for them," he said. It was the least he could do, he remarked, for my work at the awards banquet.

From the market, I hadn't clip-clopped more than six steps toward my bike when I encountered Cory. Had he been following me?

"Hey, Ronnie," he crowed. "I want to talk to you."

While I prepared to turn and run, I forged ahead with a question. "Why?"

"I can't tell you here."

I didn't have much choice, so he hopped onto the handlebars of my bike and we rode to the school yard, which, being Sunday, was locked. But we slipped in, bike and all, through an opening cut in the chain-link fence. We perched on the top of the bleachers at the baseball diamond. The white lines had been swept away by wind. A bird stood on the pitcher's mound and was joined by another bird. They were pecking at sunflower seed shells and kicking up tiny clouds of dust.

"What do you want, Cory?" I asked. "And, hey, your friends really punished me." I rolled up my sleeve and showed him a bruise the size of Texas.

"You're the only one I can talk to," Cory confided desperately. "Sorry about your bruises. I got some, too." He looked around, as if someone might overhear. "I turned thirteen today," he whispered. "Something happened."

I took a swallow of my soda and waited.

"I think I got what you got…"

A burp slowly made its way up my throat and actually fluttered my lips. I wondered what I had that made him so spooked.

"Ronnie, I think I'm a monkey like you and Joey."

A second burp followed, but this one blasted from the depths of wherever burps are created.

"Chimp, Cory," I corrected. "Not monkey. Monkeys got tails, and they're not as smart." I burped again.

Any other time, Cory would have made a nasty comment about my burp or, not to be outdone, would have produced a majestic reply. But he had grown sullen. He examined his palms, where the lines were dark and filled with sweat. He munched pensively on the inside of his cheek.

"When did it start to happen?" I asked.

"Last night. You remember how we were playing football?"

I nodded.

"I got home and was just going to eat and go to bed, but then I suddenly wanted to take a shower. I only shower three times a week, and never on Saturday."

I nodded again in sympathy.

"Like, I wanted to be clean." He wiped his palms on his pants. "Yeah, it was really strange. When I got out of the shower and looked in the mirror I saw I was a chimpanzee. I'm ugly."

I could see, in fact, some chimp features in his face. Then again, his long eyelashes reminded me of a camel. He was still evolving. "You're not that ugly," I countered, and then added, "Chimps are smart. And there are worse things."

"Like what?"

I paused before I said, "You could be a rhino like Jason."

He moaned.

"Or you could be a weasel like Robert. Or like Daniel, who's a snake and a big fat liar."

He moaned louder and kicked at a peanut shell at his feet.

We sat in silence, twin souls in rare convergence. For years Cory had bullied me and more than once hammered me into the ground like a stake. The two birds on the mound were joined by two other birds, and soon they were brawling.

"Look at 'em," I told Cory.

Cory refused and kept watching his feet.

"They're fighting like you and me and your friends." I imagined that the combative scene among the birds might bring Cory around.

More silence. The birds flew away, and wind swept the diamond. I studied my own palms with their own sweaty lines filled with dark shadows.

Our silence deepened when Cory's friends stepped through the rip in the chain-link fence. I could see that Cory was nervous that they would see us sitting together in the bleachers.

"Keep quiet," Cory whispered.

I didn't have to be told.

Jerome and Scott walked past us. They were still twelve, not ready for that big change in life. They sought the far end of the baseball diamond, where they started pushing each other and then began to wrestle in the mud. Like boys their age, they had to return home exhausted, bruised, and muddy in face, hands, and knees. They had to prove to their parents—especially their mothers—that they were still just boys.

Chapter 10

Cory and I dragged our shadows from the bleachers after Jerome and Scott left.

"I'll see you later," Cory bid in a sorrowful whisper. When he pulled his hands from his pockets to punch my forearm in friendship, they were wet with sweat. "I gotta get out of these clothes." His shirttail hung sloppily from his pants.

"Okay," I said. "Don't worry too much, Cory. It's not bad."

I risked a return home, sneaking up the lawn like a ninja. I heard Mom in the backyard, where I suspected she was splashing water on her new tomato plants. I slipped unnoticed through the front door, stripped my body of my Sunday clothes, sniffed the pile of T-shirts on my bedroom floor to find the cleanest smelling one, pushed my legs into some old pants, and tiptoed to the kitchen.

There, I opened the refrigerator and the light shone on my face. I poured a glass of pineapple smoothie, scoured the pantry for a bag of pretzels, and crept away from the house.

I had two hours before my rendezvous with Jessica. I still couldn't see Joey, who was probably wondering where I was. I was considering how to fill my time when a car pulling a trailer stopped in the middle of the street. The driver's door opened.

"Get," a voice growled as a hand deposited a small collie on the road. The door closed and the car drove off, shifting smoothly into second and third. It rattled around the corner, leaving a small puff of blue smoke hanging in the air.

I scampered up to the dog, which seemed dazed and shrunken, as if it had gone through the hot cycle of a washer.

"You okay?" I asked.

The dog's eyes were momentarily crossed. An ear was flopped in a strange way.

"You okay?" I repeated. I bent down, adjusted the ear, and let the dog sniff my hand. "Come on," I warned when I heard an approaching car. But then I recognized the car and realized that there was no danger. It was Mrs. Pinker, a widow for as long as I could remember and the granddaughter of Colonel Homer J. Pinker, founder of the town. Mrs. Pinker drove a long Oldsmobile that was responsible for most of our town's air pollution—the thing smoked like a locomotive. I led the little collie to the curb, where I checked the tags. Her name was Tammy and she lived at 237 Vine Street.

"How come they did that?" I inquired. It was a question only the owner could answer.

My mind began to spin with theories of why she had been abandoned. The owner was moving out of town—that's why the trailer was piled with stuff—and didn't want to take the dog. *What a loss,* I thought. What meanness! After all, little Tammy was young, frisky, and very polite. As distinguished ambassador for her special kind—shrunken collies—she shook my hand three times. She fetched. She rolled onto her back to bicycle her legs. She was multitalented.

"Let's see if I can get you back home."

Tammy wheeled up on her hind legs, dropped back to all fours, and trotted at my side, occasionally looking up at me in what I judged to be appreciation—no, friendship—no, just plain ol' love.

"You're such a nice dog," I cooed.

Soon we were on Vine Street, one of the rougher neighborhoods in Pinkerton. Some of the houses had cars parked on dead lawns, and porch lights were on in the middle of the day. At one house, long-neglected Christmas tree lights hung sloppily from eaves and were winking pale, anemic colors. The door, I noticed, was open and slipping off its hinges. Within its walls beat heavy metal music. At another house, a blanket was hung like drapes on the front window. And was that a toilet sitting on the porch? A baby sat in a rusty swing—no, it was just a plastic doll with its eyes closed.

I located the house. The door was open and flies, like sentries, guarded its entry.

"Hello?" I called nervously from the porch. "Hello? Hello?" I pushed the doorbell, but it failed to ring. My heart beat hard. I swatted away a few muscular flies struggling to use my nose as a resting spot.

Tammy entered the house barking her hello.

"Tammy!" I called frantically. "Get out of there." I slapped my thighs and clicked my tongue as I beckoned her. I finally trumpeted through cupped hands, "Come on, Tammy! Get out of there."

But Tammy disappeared into one of the rooms. I stood on the porch, boxing flies from my face and debating whether to follow. What if I had a confrontation with a toothless criminal cradling a shotgun in his tattooed arms? He would be mumbling, "Glad you came, sonny."

I took a chance. I leaned in the doorway and called, "Anybody home?"

The house creaked.

"Anybody home?" I repeated louder.

The living room was filled with a dirty couch, folding chairs, a goosenecked lamp, boxes of old clothes, three large plastic bags filled with empty beer and soda cans, stained pillows, dozens of coffee cans set against a far wall, and just plain trash. The place held the smell of abandonment.

I entered by taking one long, careful step, and then another.

"Where are you?" I called. "Tammy, where are you?" I tiptoed to the kitchen, where I discovered her licking a dry plastic dish. "Tammy!" I called. "Come on, let's go, girl."

We peeled out of that house and went back to the market, where I bought a single can of food for my new friend. Outside, at the curb where pigeons congregated, I pulled the tab lid and the fragrance of meat had Tammy prancing in place.

"He's cute," Jessica cried joyfully.

"She," I corrected. "Her name is Tammy." I explained how she had been abandoned.

"Oh, that's cruel." Jessica petted Tammy's fur

and gave her a big hug. "Poor Tammy." Then she asked, "Are you going to keep her?"

"If my mom lets me."

Four o'clock had finally come, and we were seated on Jessica's front lawn. Her mother was washing the front window with a garden hose. It was time to wipe away the winter grime.

"I'll take her, if you can't." Jessica turned her head and for a brief moment watched her mother as she stepped down from a stepladder. "If Mom lets me."

It was time to reveal why I wanted to speak with her. I hadn't practiced a speech about Joey's finer points, such as his wrestling moves and his loyalty to friends, but I had assumed my words would flow brilliantly.

I started: "Iyakindalikeyouknowjoeymyrealgood-friendyouknowwegottoschoolandwellkindaIya-wantto—"

"What are you saying?" Jessica laughed with her hand over her mouth. "You are so funny."

"I'm saying, Iyakindalikeyouknowlikalikajoeyis-reallycool." I had turned to jelly, weak of body and mind, and I was rushing my words. It was awkward to declare my best friend's romantic intentions. No, nearly impossible. Also, I was scared that Joey might get mad at me for telling. I would have to make Jessica guess what I couldn't say. Maybe charades would get my meaning across. Jessica kindly got me started.

"It's about Joey, huh?"

I nodded and placed a hand over my heart.

"He likes the Pledge of Allegiance?" she ventured.

I hugged myself to show his loving nature.

"He's cold."

I laced my hands together and batted my eyelashes.

"He prays, huh? No, no, he's got something in his eye." She bit her lower lip as she lowered her face and thought deeply. She raised her face. "No, no, he's caught a butterfly and is about to release it!"

Frowning, I shook my head. I had done better when my hand was on my heart. I puckered up my face.

"He ate a really sour lemon?"

Here I began to hum the Beatles' "She Loves You." It was one of my mom's favorite songs. I was certain that I was doing a passable imitation when Tammy, who had been sleeping at my side, woke with a yawn. She sat up groggily, raised her nose, and howled. I decided to stop singing.

Jessica laughed and petted Tammy's snout.

"Come on, you can guess," I wheedled.

She lowered her face in thought, pulled at a handful of grass, and a minute later raised her head, flowerlike. "Joey likes me?"

I nodded rapidly. I touched my heart and threw my hands up into the sky.

"That's why he got the balloon from the rafters?"

I nodded, which provoked Tammy to nod her own shaggy head. I glowered at the dog. Was she making fun of me or trying to help me out?

"He really likes me?" Jessica asked in disbelief.

"Lots. That's why he's in the tree."

Jessica's mother called, "Young man, can you help me?"

I wanted to continue our important conversation, but I knew that good manners required me to respond. A mother was in need. I was on my feet in a flash and at her side before she got off the ladder. The front window was shiny clean and reflected the blue sky of Pinkerton. My own reflection appeared in the window. With the blue all around, with a puffy cloud in the distance, I had to admit that I wasn't such a bad-looking chimp.

"It's going to start getting warm." Jessica's mother issued this weather report as she took a few steps backward and, hand shading her eyes and on tiptoes, looked up at the roof.

I knew what was coming. Since Jessica's father

was out playing golf, I was asked in the sweetest voice if I would be so kind as to turn on the valve of the evaporator cooler.

"I would be honored," I responded courteously.

For the third time I struggled up a roof with pliers in my back pocket. The task was a cinch—it wasn't necessary to use the pliers. I just twisted the valve and the sound of water filled the copper tubing. *Mission accomplished,* I thought, and stood for a minute, hands on hips, admiring the view.

She's coming, Joey! I shouted in my imagination. *She'll be there soon.*

Jessica and her mom were watching from down below. I felt bravery circulating in my blood. Courage, too, and vision! I stared far into the distance. Macho me, I puffed out my chest, and here is where I went wrong, because the expansion of my puny rib cage shifted my balance. Two shingles peeled away from their tacks and once again I found myself sliding toward the edge. This time I didn't panic. I raised my hands for balance, bent my knees, and kept my body loose as I sailed from the roof with two shingles plastered to the bottoms of my shoes. Like a cat, I had lost another life, but I had six more.

"That was great!" Jessica screamed in admiration. "You should go out for gymnastics."

"Are you okay?" Jessica's mom asked.

"Yeah, I think so." I kicked the shingles from my soles.

Jessica's mom disappeared into the house and returned with glasses of lemonade, my reward for hard work. Jessica and I enjoyed our drinks on the front lawn. My legs buzzed from my fall and Jessica's heart, I could see, was fluttering. She was telling me about her first gymnastics competition when she was six, but I sensed that she was dwelling on my amigo, Joey.

"I have to show you something!" she said suddenly.

"What?"

She jumped to her feet, ran inside, and returned with her hands behind her back, concealing what I hoped was a banana or apple. Those pretzels I had devoured an hour ago were nothing but a pile of sawdust in my stomach.

"I saved it," Jessica claimed as she sat down, legs crossing effortlessly. "The balloon."

Most of the helium was gone, but it was still plump as a squash. I was delighted. This was the love object that had brought them together, a sacred keepsake that cost next to nothing. A penny, maybe? But the memories!

"You like him, too?" I asked boldly.

She pulled a handful of grass from the lawn and

threw the clippings into the air. "I don't know. He's kinda cute."

Cute, I thought. *Joey is cute?*

"He's really brave, too. I bet he would have been great in gymnastics."

"Why don't you call him?" I gave her the number to his mom's cell phone.

She hid her giggly smile behind her hand.

"He'll like it. He's got nothing to do but listen to birds in the trees." This was an outright lie because I knew Joey was living like a king among those leafy branches.

Jessica pulled at a patch of grass around her feet until that part of the lawn was nearly bald. "Can I tell you something?" she asked.

I was accustomed to no one ever telling me anything. I was riveted to hear her secret.

"I'm going to quit gymnastics and get into cheer."

I tried to look delighted.

"What do you think of that?"

I swallowed and timidly asked, "Jessica, what do you mean 'cheer'?"

Her mouth opened in disbelief, revealing a wad of blue gum. She flicked a handful of grass at me. "It's cheerleading. I can't believe you! Cheer is like when you have a football team and they're down one hundred ten to three. The cheerleaders get out there and rev up the team when they're down."

"Oh, them," I remarked lightly, realizing that cheerleading was Jessica's new passion. "Oh, my gosh, how did the team get down one hundred ten to three?"

Jessica bellowed that I was dumb, but good dumb. I gave the whole situation some serious consideration. It seemed that Jessica was quitting gymnastics and Joey no longer wrestled.

"Hmmm," I murmured. In one of the myriad folds of my brain, I secreted a tactic for bringing them together. Could Jessica and Joey be a team— a cheerleading team? I imagined Joey letting Jessica stand on his strong shoulders and flipping her through the air.

From the phone at Jessica's house, I called Joey.

"Joey, it's me," I barked brightly. In the background I could hear a blender whizzing at an incredible force. He was concocting an afternoon smoothie. My stomach growled.

"Ronnie!" Joey yelled. The blender stopped. "Where are you? You want to come over for a smoothie? I've been playing chess."

Joey had gotten a computer chess game for his

thirteenth birthday and had yet to win against this mighty competitor. "I finally won!" he bragged with pride.

"Shut up!"

"Yeah, I did. Honest!"

I congratulated him. I'd be there in a flash, I promised, and asked him to please save some smoothie for me.

Jessica got permission to go see Joey—the boy in the tree, as her mother described him. On the walk to Joey's house, we decided to play the game of seeing how long we could keep the balloon in the air.

"Don't let it fall!" Jessica screamed.

The balloon was semideflated, and I patted it artfully. Jessica, a true athlete, kept the balloon from touching the ground several times. Thus, we marched over to Joey's house, full of happiness, and laughing when Tammy saved us from certain death—we pretended the balloon was a bomb—by poking it back into the air.

Chapter 11

"Life is a crooked road," my mother would cry when something went wrong—the day Dad hopped into that woman's sports car being the most recent. But I always wondered what she meant by "a crooked road." Mom included everything from plumbing problems to runs in her stockings to cheese gone moldy. "Crooked road," she complained from her recliner after a hard day working at the grocery store. "Life is a crooked road—you'll see!" I didn't dare point out that Pinkerton was built on straight lines, not like those winding one-lane cobbled roads in Europe. How could we really experience this crooked road business?

But I began to grasp Mom's meaning when Jessica, Tammy, and I were playfully tapping the balloon with our fingertips, knuckles, shoulders, heads, knees, and, in Tammy's case, wet snout. We were determined to see Joey right away, but in my path—on the crooked road—a kid of about four was crying in the middle of the sidewalk. We could have crossed the street, but that would have avoided fate or, at least, made me a coward. I was shocked to see that the little boy was sitting on my old trike! Had it already been sold at the rummage sale? We stopped to see.

"What's wrong?" Jessica asked. She bent down and placed her hands on the handlebars. Tammy, in turn, sniffed the front and back wheels.

"Boots!" Hot tears ran down his face.

"Tell me what's wrong," Jessica cooed.

"Boots." The boy pointed a sticky finger at the roof of a house, where a kitten was meowing.

I had been in such a good mood, but now I was worried. Was it fate that I should lose another life if I had to climb to the roof?

"How did it get up there?" Jessica cooed even more sweetly.

"Don't know!" the boy cried. He got off my trike—his, I mean—and crumpled on the front lawn.

I assumed that the boy had let the kitten run out of the house, and maybe the springy legs of this kitten had brought it face-to-face with the daffodils, the garden hose and sprinkler, a snail with its big shell of goo, and finally the ladder leaning against the house. That must have been how the kitten climbed onto the roof.

"I like your trike," I told the kid. "I had one just like that." I didn't say the trike once belonged to me, but I could have offered proof. I could have rolled up my pants and showed him the array of scars on my knees. And too bad I wasn't home where I could go into my sock drawer and show him the baby tooth that got knocked out when I tipped the trike over.

The child quietly stopped sobbing when I got onto the trike and rode up and down his driveway, goofily tipping it over but righting it quickly and saying, "Oops, but I'm not hurt." This brought sunshine to the boy's face. It also brought out his sister, who asked nastily, "What are you doing?" She was about fifteen, her face colored brightly with makeup. There was no sunshine on her face. She seemed plain hard.

Jessica stepped in and took the child's hand in hers. "Hi, Alyssa," she said. "Your brother was crying. Your cat's on the roof."

I assumed that Jessica knew the girl from gymnastics, as the girl was slender but bulky in the shoulders. She also sported a ponytail, like Jessica.

"What?" Alyssa stepped off the porch. Walking backward, her hand over her brow in a sort of salute, she spied the roof. When she saw Boots she narrowed her eyes at her brother.

"Did you throw her up there?" she asked angrily.

I took a step back at the possibility that the kid might have thrown the kitten onto the roof. To me, he looked sweet. But you could never tell.

He shook his head.

"Then how did he get up there?"

"He climbed," the boy whimpered.

Since I was experienced with roofs, both in the climbing and falling, I boldly made a suggestion to end this drama. "It's a piece of cake. I'll get her."

I climbed the ladder, dusted off my palms as I stood up, and called, "kittykittykitty."

The kitten meowed twice, hissed, and ran away.

"Come on, little kitty." I got down on all fours. I meowed like a cat, but that made the cat freak out and scamper to the other end of the roof. So I played bad cop and patrolled the roof from one corner to another until the cat hissed, revealed its claws, and puffed up its tail. But once I had it in my arms, the kitten gave up and began to purr.

"You naughty Boots!" I scolded playfully.

To my amazement I descended the ladder without harm. But when I touched ground and handed Boots to the child my heart almost stopped.

A familiar truck rolled up the driveway, and we had to move out of the way. It revved its engine and cut off, the exhaust pipe popping and hurling black smoke. The door opened and out stepped one of the teenagers who had stolen my bike. He was smirking at me.

"So, how was church?" he asked.

"It was good." I swallowed and almost braved, "I like your singing." That comment probably would have made him punch me in the nose, or at least stomp on the tips of my shoes—he stood that close to me.

He stepped up to Alyssa and gave her a peck on the mouth. I was amazed. It sort of made me sick, as this kiss between them made the slurping suction sound you get when you unplug the drain in the kitchen sink.

"How's my girl?" he asked, his hand around her waist. More sickness churned in my stomach.

"Okay," she said. "You know Jessica?"

"Nah," he muttered. "You with this guy?" He pointed a hitchhiker's thumb at me.

"We're friends," Jessica answered.

I could see that Jessica didn't think much of

Alyssa's boyfriend. The teenager—Eric, we learned—kissed Alyssa a second time. He was just a big mean lug, but I was resolved not to tell Jessica how he had stolen my bike and how I'd miraculously retrieved it from church. Snitching on him wasn't worth it.

"How you like your trike?" Eric asked.

The child gripped the handlebars and lowered his face.

"Tell Eric 'Thank you,'" Alyssa scolded.

"Thank you," the boy whispered and pedaled away, a sign that we should leave, too.

"We got to go," I said and laughed.

"What's so funny?" Eric edged toward me.

I erased the smile from my face. When I saw his mouth bend into a crooked shape, I thought of Mom and her assertion that life was at times a crooked road. It could also be full of crooked mouths.

"You hear me?" More crooked mouth.

"Leave him alone," Alyssa warned. "Don't be like that."

"Heard your friend's up a tree—man!" he said. "Don't he got a home?"

I was amazed by the crookedness of the finger he pointed at me.

"Yeah, he's got a home. He just likes it up there."

"Is he a monkey or something?" Crooked mouth again.

"No, he's not a monkey."

"Stop it!" Alyssa scolded her boyfriend playfully. "Let's go inside." She had picked up the kitten and pressed it to her heart.

"Come on," Jessica said as she glared at Eric and pulled on my arm.

I was a little scared of getting hit by him, but there was another emotion percolating inside me. I was sadder that my trike was gone from my life. The boy seemed deserving of a trike, but he didn't know that Eric had probably copped it from a church. I was sure he had given it to the little boy to get on the good side of Alyssa. But as I walked away with Tammy on my left and Jessica on my right, I wondered how much of a good side Alyssa had.

"Don't feel bad," Jessica cooed.

We had returned to batting the balloon in the air, but it was I who failed to keep it afloat. My mood had darkened.

"I can't help it," I replied. "He's a bully. Just because he has a truck!"

I scratched Tammy's head and hoped that I could live up to what my new dog thought of me. Why couldn't I be brave instead of a wimp pushed around by a bully? A bully who was also a thief!

"Alyssa's not nice either." Jessica released a sigh. "I know you're feeling bad."

"I am," I admitted. I was tired of my role as Cupid and tired of climbing onto roofs and turning on valves and rescuing cats.

We stood in silence, or near silence, as Tammy had cornered a flea in her shoulder and was attacking it with chomping teeth.

"Let me show you something," Jessica said after a while. She pulled on my arm and started in a direction that wouldn't lead us to Joey's place.

"What about Joey?" I was determined to deliver Jessica to Joey and then go my own way, which for me would be a Sunday meal and an hour of *Animal Planet*. "Don't you want to see him?"

"He's not going anywhere," she retorted. "You said he's not coming down."

We hurried six blocks to the industrial part of Pinkerton and stopped in front of an abandoned broom factory. A portion of the roof was missing and through these holes birds entered and exited. A stray cat lurked near an oil barrel. And were those bats hanging in the eaves?

"I remember this place," I remarked. "They gave away a bunch of brooms when they shut down. We got red ones."

"My grandfather started the factory."

"No!"

"He did. He made brooms that went all over the place. In fact, when I went to see the *Queen Mary* in Long Beach, I saw one of his brooms. A sailor was using it."

"Wow," I uttered. It struck me as amazing that all the things made in this town—brooms, baseball caps, computers, or boxes of raisins—could circle the globe.

We ducked our heads and scooted through the chain-link fence. We walked around the outer grounds of the factory. A couple of rusty trucks sat with flat tires in the shadow of a tall smokestack. A rusty gasoline pump looked ready to fall over.

"That's where they put the straw," Jessica pointed out. "And that's where they lay my dog when he got killed. That's what Dad said."

I eyed Jessica, confused. I was suddenly over-whelmed by the smell of hay, though the pile that filled the bin was mushy in its state of de-composition.

"My dad used to be the foreman here." She pet-ted Tammy, who had sidled up next to her. "He used to take Mercury—that was my dog—to work. One day, Mercury got killed when a roll of baling wire fell on him."

I swallowed and wasn't sure what to say. I had

lost a cat once—to old age—and had begun to understand mortality when one morning I found my hamster, Melvin, on his back, with his eyes open and sort of grinning. I had lost a lot of playground fights. But a dog getting killed? And in an accident? That would be the worst.

"He was a great dog. He could swim." Jessica described how she and Mercury would paddle in Bass Lake. He was also the perfect alarm clock. In the mornings, she recalled with a big smile, he scratched at her bedroom door at exactly a quarter to seven. And for comfort, what was a better shoulder than a dog's?

"Poor Mercury," I said. At that moment I wished I had had a dog when I was little. "How old was he?"

"Six, I think. He was so cute."

I observed a roll of baling wire next to the bin where straw was kept. I wondered whether it was the same roll that had killed Mercury. I wondered whether his body was buried near the factory, or maybe in her backyard.

"I know that Eric pushing you around and Mercury getting killed like that are different." Jessica wasn't making sense. She tried again. "Eric is a lot of hot air and can hurt your feelings, but when your dad comes home to tell you that your dog is dead, it's way worse."

This was an improvement in logic, and I could see her point. I could also feel the pumps behind my eyes preparing to spill tears. I choked. I had never really talked with a girl before, but now I was convinced they were more sensitive.

"I agree," I responded meekly and turned away to rake a tear from my eye.

"Mercury used to like to go hiking." Jessica began to ruffle Tammy's fur in affection. "But he wasn't much of a guard dog. He liked people too much."

"You loved him a lot, huh?"

"A lot."

I sighed. Jessica's memory of Mercury was making her sad. And the memory of what Eric had done was making me sad. I wished I had one of Jessica's grandfather's brooms to sweep those feelings away. Wishful thinking.

In the real world, Eric was a bully and bullies ruled schools, but eventually they went away and sometimes they had their lights punched out by someone who was bigger and badder. This much I knew. Uncle Vic had told me so, and so had my mom when I came home one day holding my nose. I recalled that bloody-nose day because Mom had lamented, "Life is full of crooked roads." She peeked at my nose and added, "And crooked noses!"

"Come on—let's go!" Jessica beckoned. She wiped her eyes and reached into her pocket for a Kleenex. "Let's be happy."

Tammy barked and pranced.

"See—Tammy wants to go," Jessica said. "You lead the way, girl."

We picked up the scent of our purpose, which was to see Joey, himself hurting from a stinging insult. Jessica began to bat the balloon again, and this time we kept it in the air with every possible part of our bodies, plus Tammy's snout. The balloon dropped several times, but we didn't mind.

Chapter 12

When we arrived, victorious in our efforts to keep the balloon afloat, we found Joey's mom squandering her time knitting. It looked like a baby sweater. She was seated in a lawn chair near Joey's tree, the webbed bottom of the chair sagging from the weight of years.

"Hello, Mrs. Rios," I hailed. "What are you knitting?"

"Coat for Rex."

I thought of Tyrannosaurus rex and the miles of yarn it would take to cover that monster. I asked, "Who's Rex?"

She explained that it was her friend's Chihuahua. Then she asked, "And who do we have here?"

"This is Jessica. She wanted to see Joey."

Jessica whispered, "Hi."

I was surprised that Jessica spoke in a near

mumble. Just minutes before, she had preached such a strong message about bullies. She had seemed so confident that as we rolled through life all the hard edges would smooth out. Now her demeanor had completely changed—she seemed bashful as a lamb.

"Jessica does gymnastics," I said.

"Have you been doing gymnastics long, dear?" Joey's mom asked. I noticed that her knitting had increased in speed.

"Since I was six." Jessica's smile was genuine.

"You must be about...thirteen."

"Gee, everyone seems to be thirteen," I remarked lamely. I got the feeling that Joey's mom was suspicious of Jessica. I had to work myself into the conversation to keep it from being a showdown: overprotective mother versus the new girl. "I mean, Cory turned thirteen today, too. Isn't that something?"

They ignored me.

Joey's mom asked, "Do you know my son Joey?"

"Sort of. He doesn't go to the same school as me. But I met him Friday night."

I shoved my way into the conversation. "Hey, guess what I did today?"

Mrs. Rios ignored me again. She raised her head

and called, "Joey, are you going to come down? It's almost dinnertime."

The leaves rustled, but, otherwise, there was no response.

"He's so stubborn," Mrs. Rios stated. She said that she had been trying to coax Joey down so he could get a good night's sleep for school tomorrow.

I needed to turn the conversation away from Joey and Jessica to keep Mrs. Rios off the scent. I figured I was a pretty good conversation piece and announced, "I went to church today, Mrs. Rios."

It appeared that I was invisible.

"Joey is so stubborn," Mrs. Rios repeated. "But a good boy."

"I'm sure he is," Jessica agreed. "He's Ronnie's best friend, and Ronnie is, like, really super."

"Jessica and I go way back," I lied as I stumped for attention. "Hey, Mrs. Rios, this is my dog, Tammy."

Mrs. Rios cut her eyes to me and then lowered them to Tammy.

"She was sort of abandoned." I ruffled Tammy's head and my new dog looked up, the bud of her tongue showing. She was way cute!

Joey's mom unexpectedly halted her inquisition. She rose from her chair and sniffed the air—smoke was drifting over the roof from a barbecue in the backyard. "I've got to check on Alex." Mr. Rios considered himself a grill master, though undercooked chicken and burned steaks were his specialty. Joey's mom excused herself and left, her slippers spanking her heels.

"Gosh, she asked a lot of questions," Jessica remarked. "I don't know if she likes me."

"She likes you. I know she does." I was going to point out that Mrs. Rios was just being an overprotective mother when the tree began to rustle and shake violently. It seemed as if the tree was going to send Joey catapulting into the next yard. Then, to my shock, I glimpsed Coach Bear climbing awkwardly down the rope ladder. When he was inches from the ground, he let go, landed with a thud that buckled his knees, then turned and hitched up his pants.

"Coach!" I cried.

"Ronnie," he said matter-of-factly. "I thought Joey's mom would never leave. I have been up there for almost an hour. I'd hate for anyone to see an old guy like me up in a tree."

"Are things cool between you and Joey?" I asked.

He said that he had apologized to Joey and begged him to please come down.

"Gosh, that's great, Coach." I was happy that he was not just a grumpy hairy bear, but a good guy who could fathom the hurt soul of a teenager. He was tenderhearted after all!

"I've seen you before," Coach Bear greeted Jessica, who had sidled up next to me.

"I got a gymnastics award on Friday night."

Coach Bear pounded his forehead with his palm. "Oh, yeah, dumb me, I forgot." He congratulated her again and mentioned he had a date. He had fish to fry and someone to share it with.

Coach Bear wasn't more than a dozen steps from his adios when Joey called from the tree, "Ronnie! Ronnie, come up here!" I caught sight of him nervously peering down through the branches. "Ronnie, get up here!"

I climbed the rope ladder.

"She's really here?" Joey cried nervously. He was on the verge of hyperventilating, and I felt it was my duty to calm him down. For a second I thought of throwing water into his face. But I decided to ply him with soothing words.

"Yeah, Jessica's here," I said. "Just relax. Be your usual self."

At the mention of her name, his cheeks reddened. He gazed shyly down at his feet. It took a few minutes for him to reclaim a hold on himself, during which time I snagged a banana and unzipped it artfully with a fingernail. I would devour that mushy sweetness in three bites.

"Jessica!" I trumpeted. "Come on up." My attention fell briefly on Tammy, who was drinking from the dripping garden hose. "Tammy, don't go anywhere." Tammy looked up, drops of water clinging to her whiskers.

Jessica climbed into the tree. At the sight of her, Joey's face turned even redder—heck, he was looking like a ripe plum! It was Jessica's turn to blush and shyly regard her feet. Was this the start of love? In my mind, I pulled back Cupid's bow and slaughtered them really good. Surely they had already started liking each other. What would Joey's mother think of that?

"Hi," began Joey. Some of the red left his cheeks and traveled to me. It was funny seeing Joey so nervous. Even I was embarrassed.

"Hi," Jessica whispered in return.

"Hi," he repeated.

Jessica presented him with the balloon, which she had been holding behind her back. "Remember this?"

Joey's eyes became coins of light. Dang, he was expressing all the signs of love! From the look of things, it was only a matter of seconds before he would float into the air.

"I remember it," he replied. "You're a really great athlete."

"Oh, stop it. You are! You were so awesome climbing way up there to get the balloon." She tucked a loose strand of hair behind her ear. "I couldn't do what you did."

I pushed into the conversation. "Do you know that trees are thirstier than humans? They're thirstier than dogs and cats put together." I wasn't sure if this last statement could be backed up by science, but it sounded plausible. After all, cats and dogs are smaller than your average tree.

They both ignored me.

"Climbing up there like that was really something," Jessica gushed with a huge smile. "That was, like, *so* super!"

"Ah, thanks," Joey replied, red spots glowing on his cheeks.

I had had enough.

"Joey!" I barked at my friend.

"What?"

"I was surprised to see Coach Bear."

The red spots on his cheeks paled.

"Yeah, he told me how sorry he was."

"That was nice of him, don't you think?"

"Yeah. He says he's going to try to get me rein-stated next year if I want to wrestle."

Coach Bear was a champ of a person. For Joey, wrestling was not only the best sport in the world, but one you could put to use if someone pushed you around. Then I noticed Joey had turned goofy again. His smile was off center.

"Joey, show Jessica around. Give her a tour of your kingdom."

Joey, a congenial host, was happy to offer a tour of the first level. But first we drank a blueberry smoothie and topped that off with handfuls of al-monds and walnuts. We sat cross-legged on a rug as we got comfortable. I began our conversation by saying that green was my favorite color. Joey, who had returned some of his attention to me, crowed, "Green is my favorite color, too."

We two amigos explored our penchant for the color green. Green was the color of grass and we liked to wrestle in grass and sometimes just park our bodies on grass. Green was the color of a lot of vegetables—artichokes, asparagus, broccoli, peas. We revisited the day we became vegetarians after watching a program on *Animal Planet* about an or-phaned lamb. We debated how to make the best smoothies in the world.

Jessica was a good listener. She cut her eyes to Joey when he pontificated with expressive gestures, and then she swiveled her attention to me when I bragged about our culinary skills.

"You guys are so much fun," Jessica praised. We blushed. "You are two of a kind."

"That's right!" Joey blared. He went on to talk about our bad side, such as when we had written our names in wet cement.

But for me the conversation stopped when I caught sight of a cinder, red as evil, floating through the air and settling on the wood-shingled roof of the Rios house. The cinder had floated from the backyard, where the grill was.

"I got to go do something," I told them.

"What?"

I remembered Joey. I remembered the awards banquet and how he had leaped to his feet and become a hero. Couldn't I do the same? Would some cute girl see me?

"Something," I answered vaguely. I slithered down the rope ladder and ran to the house with Tammy on my heels. I looked for a way to boost myself up and saw a wooden ladder lying in the bushes. I pulled, dragged, and set the ladder against the house. I was up on the roof in a flash. As I waved at

Joey and Jessica in the tree, I realized that both their names began with a J. Was it a coincidence? Or cosmic? Would I find a Rebecca or a Rachael?

But I had no time to ponder my future love life because a breeze had breathed on the cinder, setting a shingle on fire. It was sort of like a small campfire—flames leaping but not high. I started stomping, jumping up and down on the flames, rubbing them with the soles of my shoes and even spitting at them.

After I crushed the fire, I stood on that shingle to smother it for good. I could feel some heat in my shoes, but I was determined to conquer that trouble spot on the roof.

"What's going on up there?" Joey's mom was gazing up at me. She was holding a skewer of vegetable shish kebab—how sweet she was to remember that Joey and I were vegetarians.

"It's a small fire, Mrs. Rios," I yelled. "Don't worry. I put it out already." I felt like a hero and even envisioned my photo in the newspaper. I saw myself being presented with a gift certificate and a bronze plaque. And was that me at the wheel of Pinkerton's fire engine?

To further demonstrate my heroics, I started stomping on the smoldering shingle, a mistake because I lost my balance, fell on my rump, and started skidding off the roof. *Yikes,* I whimpered. *Here I go again.* Once again, I saw my life flash past me— Joey and I in our strollers, the day at the zoo with Mom and my deadbeat dad, my trike, my first bike, a heaping pile of Sacagawea dollar coins, my two years in Little League, my one year of really bad soccer, again my trike, bowls and bowls of bananas and apples, again my first bike but this time in the back of that mean teenager's truck. I saw my life whiz past and in those seconds I realized that maybe Mom was right when she said that life is short. But could it be this short?

As I flew off the roof, I caught sight of Tammy. She was gnawing at a flea on her shoulder and seemed indifferent to my possible demise. I had time to see Joey and Jessica in the tree, their mouths open as I fell. I had time to see Mrs. Rios who was holding up that skewer of vegetables—my reward for a flight more dangerous than gymnastics, perhaps even more gutsy than a thirteen-second pin in wrestling. I gulped. I winced. I sucked in a lungful of air, and realized that I had done at least one thing memorable in my thirteen years: I had brought Joey and Jessica together.

Like a cat, I landed on my feet. But like a gymnast I then dropped and rolled, gathering up grass and creating a dizzy spin inside my head. Tammy barked and wagged at my accomplishment.

"Ronnie, are you okay?" Mrs. Rios asked.

I staggered to my feet, brushed myself off, and let Tammy lick my fingers, which burned with pain from splinters.

"Yeah, I'm talented at falling off roofs."

Mrs. Rios handed me the skewer and disappeared into the house for rubbing alcohol and tweezers to yank out my splinters with.

I sat down on the lawn, where I nibbled the middle goodies on the skewer—the roasted tomatoes first, followed by what I discovered were chunks of zucchini—and then jerked out of that tasty experience when I heard Joey cry, "Are you okay?"

I got to my feet, churning the food in my mouth. I swallowed. "Yeah, I'm okay."

"Was that a fire?" Jessica asked.

I could see her pants legs but not the rest of her. She and Joey were still way up in the branches.

"Yeah, it was."

Joey told me that I was really brave and announced that he would be coming down from the tree.

"Take your time." I needed to enjoy that skewer. As I devoured the tasty veggies, I came to understand that I had matured. I dabbed the corners of my mouth with the napkin Mrs. Rios had handed me. When I burped, I said, "Excuse me." I was a